Tales From Stonecutter Street

Other books by F. W. Thomas:

Extra Turns (1917)
Saturday Nights (1923)
Low and I: A Cooked Tour in London (1923)
Merry Go Round (1924)
Rain and Shine (1924)
Cobbler's Wax (1925)
The Low and I Holiday Book (1925)
Week-Ends (1925)
All A-Blowing (1927)
Windfalls (1932)
The Merrygo Almanack (1933)
The Ballads of Barnacle Bill and Other Jingles (1943)

Tales From Stonecutter Street

Other books by F. W. Thomas:

Extra Turns (1917)
Saturday Nights (1923)
Low and I: A Cooked Tour in London (1923)
Merry Go Round (1924)
Rain and Shine (1924)
Cobbler's Wax (1925)
The Low and I Holiday Book (1925)
Week-Ends (1925)
All A-Blowing (1927)
Windfalls (1932)
The Merrygo Almanack (1933)
The Ballads of Barnacle Bill and Other Jingles (1943)

Tales From Stonecutter Street

F. W. Thomas

Edited by Richard Simms

Richard Simms Publications

This paperback first edition published in 2010

Richard Simms Publications, Surrey, England

ISBN: 978-0-9556942-5-7

The articles and sketches in this collection were originally published in the *Morning Leader* newspaper between 1905 and 1912.

With special thanks to Sue Wakefield, Morgan Wallace, Robin Andrews, David Andrews and Wendy Marriott.

For more information please visit the F. W. Thomas web page:

http://thestarfictionindex.atwebpages.com/f_w.htm

Contents

Introduction

One of the most popular English humorists of his day, F. W. Thomas (1882-1966) wrote hundreds of stories, sketches, poems and articles for the London evening newspaper *The Star*. His outstanding copy appeared regularly in that publication for over three glorious decades, entertaining generations of Londoners. Several book collections of Thomas' work for *The Star* were published during the course of his career and were met with critical acclaim. These highly collectible books include volumes such as *Extra Turns* (1917), *Saturday Nights* (1923) and *Windfalls* (1932).

But an earlier series of articles originally published in the *Morning Leader* were never reprinted in book form. Recently rediscovered, Thomas' complete writings for this newspaper have now been assembled in one volume. "Tales From Stonecutter Street" brings together the varied and interesting stories, sketches and essays that Thomas contributed to the *Morning Leader* between 1905 and 1912. All but the first three of these were written while Thomas was employed as a junior reporter in the newspaper's offices in Stonecutter Street. Under the guidance and encouragement of editor Ernest Parke, Thomas produced an impressive string of miscellaneous pieces that serve as evidence of a budding talent coming to fruition.

In this book you will find a number of sketches about London life in the Edwardian era. Whether they are about searching for a job, the travails of commuting to the City on overcrowded rush-hour trains, the dreaded annual office party, or the gentler reflections on his childhood that Thomas was apt to make on his customary walks along the Embankment, these perceptive pieces, by turns funny or poignant, cynical or reassuring, still resonate a century later. The modern reader will certainly find much to relate to, and laugh about, in the observational sketches and articles contained in these pages.

Also included here are a series of informal essays that provide the reader with sprinklings of social commentary, dealing with such commonplace subjects as people's dining habits, the "art" of wearing clothes, and admiring the displays in shop windows. Thomas' keen observations on the social mannerisms and conventions of the time are highlighted in these insightful and humorous articles.

In this unique collection, the reader will encounter some early examples of Thomas' delightful countryside yarns, in which he lovingly describes, with a poetic intensity, the beauty of Nature and the changing of the seasons. Thomas documents with both charm and clarity his various hikes across the Sussex Downs and Surrey Hills and woodlands. At times these beguiling passages have a surreal, dream-like quality, as when Thomas follows a certain blackbird for many miles along the Pilgrims' Way, or listens to the song of a nightingale during a memorable nocturnal stroll he once took along a riverbank.

Whatever their subject, the pieces assembled in "Tales From Stonecutter Street" compare favourably with his later writings, and are accomplished works in their own right. These "lost" early sketches show a major talent emerging into the literary firmament, and exhibit an unusual maturity and depth for a young writer.

Richard Simms
Surrey, England
February, 2010

On Getting the Sack

By a Clerk.

"—And so I think it will be better for us both if we part this day month."

Thus "the Governor," and thanking him, I left the presence.

This was the penalty, then, a month's notice. The crime would not be understood by the lay reader, and, anyhow, it does not matter.

When I left the *sanctum sanctorum* I was using my thinking apparatus at about ten thousand horse-power. (My late boss would have said donkey-power, but his opinion doesn't count.) Was it true? Was I really sacked? I thought of all the plans I had made, now hopelessly disarranged. There was that new overcoat, such a nice grey I had chosen; there was my season ticket, with six weeks still unexpired; there was that little treat, an evening at His Majesty's, that I had promised myself on pay-day. There was—oh, there were a heap of things all cut and dried, and now—there was the sack. It never struck me to think, at least not then, of the more vital points; whether I should get another crib before I left, what I was going to do while out, etc.

Have you ever been out of work? If not, don't try it in order to verify what I say, as you mightn't get in again. It's a rather peculiar experience.

You go to the office on the 30th as usual, arriving five minutes late, also as usual, and you leave in the evening, saying good-bye all round. Next morning you wake up and gaze gloomily at your watch. (I wonder where that watch is now. I never paid any interest on the ticket.) Half-past seven. So you draw your knees up to your chin, and think over the day's work. Let's see, there are those railway accounts to pass, the bought ledger wants casting, and, and—you sit up with a jerk just to make sure you are awake. Then it all rushes on you. Why, you're sacked! You're out of work! And a still small voice whispers the consoling information, "and you're free."

Yes, you're free! and it's chilly sitting up in bed, so you get down again, right down, and go through it all once more. What are you going to do?

The sun is beckoning through the window, making the room look warm. You get up, wash, "brekker," and take up the paper to look down the advertisements. The sun is still beckoning you out. Nothing but agencies and spare-time swindles, so you throw the paper aside, and finish your breakfast.

Now for it! You will go to one or two employment bureaux, and put your name on their books. You will go to the Guildhall Library and see the "Public Ledger." The sun still beckons. You will write to this man and that man. And still the sun is beckoning. It's all over. The sun has won. You put on your old biking knickers, take a cap and a stick, and go out. Epping Forest is only about forty minutes' walk, and you do it in thirty.

Your spirits are boylike. You want to run. The roads are open and hard. There is a glorious breeze across the fields. The trees are showering their offerings of gorgeous-coloured leaves at the feet of a departing summer, and all Nature is singing a requiem. But half a minute! Is it a requiem? It ought to be. It's October, autumn.

No, it's a Song of Spring, an awakening! Look at the blue sky, the scudding wisps of silvery cloud. Look at the dry, frosty road. If you thought no one were looking you'd go down that hill like Watling-st. Brigade down Ludgate-hill.

As you walk over the springy turf, smiting fallen acorns with your stick, you think of Mincing-lane, with its relentless clamour of cabs, hawkers, brokers, paper boys, and vendors of the "always 'andy" article. You look, mentally, into the office so lately left, and see Grant growling over his day-books, King cursing his bills of lading, Farmer fuming at his bank round. You think of the rush and the worry that thousands of men are making of life in the Babylon behind you. The lines they draw on their faces, the smuts they make on their souls, the endless striving, struggling, driving, wrecking, and all for what? Happiness? No, all for money! You think of the sweater and sweated,

12

the man who earns and does not get, and he who gets and does not earn, and you wonder why they keep on.

Why don't they come out here in God's open air and live clean? Yes, that's the secret. Out here one could live clean, but behind it's all smoke and soot, money and want of it, cursing and closing prices, falling markets and fallen men.

That's how you feel about it, and you wish you might leave it all, and go back to the land there is so much talk about. But you are not alone in the matter; there are others concerned, and it would not do.

Besides (oh! the bathos of it!), what would you do with your tail-coat, top hat, tight-legged trousers, and all the other abominations of Mammon?

However, you forget it all, and make up your mind to enjoy yourself to-day, at any rate. Let to-morrow take care of—keep still, there's a rabbit. It scuttles away, its white wisp of a tail presenting a splendid mark if one were a sportsman. Overhead a robin is singing his Hymn of Praise. To-morrow he may make a dinner for a hawk, or come to some other untimely end, but he isn't looking forward to it. And that's the line you will take. Wait till it comes, and then—well, then, wait till it goes.

You find a pub, and in the sawdusted taproom order a regal meal of bread, cheese, pickles, and bitter, and this you really enjoy. You wonder who is having the better time, yourself in a common public-house (how your be-collared friends would stare!) or Jones down some smoke-laden den in the bowels of the earth, playing "fives and threes" and drinking coffee. However, at length you find yourself at home, feeling better for your day's dissipation.

On the morrow you buy your paper, and with eager eye scan the vacancy columns, and nine o'clock sees you seated before the table, paper, pen, and all the paraphernalia of the correspondent before you.

You look out of the window, suck your penholder, and wonder what Robinson is doing, what you will be doing a month hence, what the Forest is looking like. Shall you go out? Shall you go on your promised visit to the Tate Gallery? Shall you—? You resolutely dip your pen in the ink and sigh. "Sir,—In reply to your advertisement in to-day's—"

On Looking for Work

By a Clerk.

The fiat has gone forth! I have just 2s. 10d. and an empty tobacco pouch. The rest of my household gods went forth with the fiat.

How does one look for work—that is clerking—with 2s. 10d.? Of course, labouring is different. A labourer can look for work so long as he has health and two feet—though I don't say he'll find it.

The absolute uselessness of 2s. 10d. is never so evident as when it is the last 2s. 10d. you have. Then it is no good whatever. It won't nearly buy any of the things you want, and the things you don't want—well, you don't want them. However, you decide not to throw it away, for all its uselessness. You may want it later.

Now comes the domestic economy business. In order to save buying a paper (and your neighbourhood not yet having come under the eye of Mr. Carnegie) you walk to the nearest free library. This, in your instance, is the Bishopsgate Institute. Here you walk up to the newspaper room and find the reading stands surrounded by an eager throng.

You decide to wait until the crowd thins a little, and meanwhile perambulate the magazine-room. At the tables adorned with the sixpenny illustrated magazines sits a horde of not wholly desirable comrades in misfortune, who look at you as if the place belonged to them, and you were an intruder.

The next table has papers, scientific journals, of little interest to these casuals, and it is vacant but for one old man, a seedy, grey-haired, scholarly-looking man with a worried expression on his face.

On the table before him lies his battered felt hat, a motley collection of slips of paper, which you can see are covered with notes and figures, and an enormous reading-glass. He is reading an engineering journal, and occasionally jots down something on one of the slips before him. Is he a great inventor, or a crank, wasting the last few years of his life on some mad freak? But that is no concern of yours, and the crowd round the reading stands has dwindled to one, so you make your way to the papers.

You scan the "Situations vacant" from "Agencies" to "Youths," passing on the way a "volontaire" wanted, at which you grind your teeth. You ultimately bag five ads. worth answering, four of which are to go to the office of the newspaper in which they appear, and one to an address in Leadenhall-st.

Happy thought! You will write your letters in the reference library, take them to their destinations, and thus save 5d. You go out to buy paper and envelopes and hie you back. You are the only occupant of the reference library besides the attendant, so, to make things look all right, you get a book out.

Opening the card catalogue at random you strike Ovid, and apply for that gentleman's "Heroides." Going to the end of the room, you get out your paper and then make the appalling discovery that there is no ink—not a drop. Ink is prohibited, banned; there it is on the wall, writ large.

However, you are tired, and think a rest will do you good, so, turning to Ovid, you nearly get interested in the passionate epistles of Paris and Helen, Hero and Leander.

But you cannot read. A horrible gas-engine a few yards away is driving large nails into your brain with its perpetual "Teuf-teuf-spit, teuf-teuf-spit," and you *must* listen to it.

In a moment of happy inspiration you bethink you of the Guildhall Library. There you can get ink. You hasten thither, and, arrived there, are grievously disappointed to find it closed for some civic circus. You stand outside in the cold and curse Gog and Magog, Sheriffs and Councillors, Mayors and Corporations, entente cordiales, Principalities and Powers, individually and collectively, *privatim et seriatim* curse you them. May they drown in their own turtle soup! choke with their own cheddar! if they eat anything as common; hang in their own chains of office! suffocate in their own robes!

You wish you had your Ingoldsby Legends with you, that you might cull a curse from the fate of Jim Crow.

Then you feel better!

Cripplegate is the next library, and there you soon find yourself. Mustn't use ink here. Mighty careful of their musty tomes, you think. No! a clean man may not use ink, but a dirty one may wet his grimy finger when he turns a page and leave an alluvial deposit on the corner.

From Cripplegate you, doubting, journey to the office of the journal from which you have culled your advertisement. Ah! Why did not you think of this before? Here are seas of ink, forests of pens, continents of paper, bales of blotters. You write your letters, deposit the four in the box provided, bless the manager, and leave for Leadenhall-st.

Here, with a parting benediction, you launch your last argosy. Will it sink or swim? Will you get a job out of the five? With these thoughts in your head you journey wearily homewards.

Passing the Bishopsgate Institute on your way, you think to rest awhile. Everything is nearly as you left it. The crowd has changed, but it is still grimy. The bibulous magazine reader (and drinker?) is now copying out the winner and price in the 3.45 race. You hope his fancy did not get in. The gas-engine is still "teuf-teufing" outside.

You cannot stay here long; the air is foetid and vitiated, and there is a musty smell which the powerful libations of carbolic that are sprinkled around cannot entirely quench.

So, with your 2s. 10d., less the 2d. you spent on stationery, you arrive home, only to do it all over again to-morrow, without the mistakes.

On Going After a Place

By a Clerk.

"Any letters this morning, I wonder?" So you have asked yourself these last score of mornings. Morning after morning has seen you at the front window, watching for the postman, and morning after morning has seen that gentleman pass by on the other side. Some old saw-maker has said that no news is good news, but when one is out of work the monotonous reiteration of no news is bad, very bad.

You wonder whether to-day's post will break the dreary sameness.

The regulation double-bang at the door proclaims that there are certainly letters. Three altogether. One from a thoughtful friend enclosing a concert ticket (and this is corn in Egypt indeed); one from a sympathising relative proffering the now stereotyped advice to "try something else," and one, Hooray! one from a firm. "Re your application for the vacancy as clerk, please call here to-day at four o'clock. Ask for Mr. X."

Four o'clock! You have still eight hours, so you start getting ready at once.

Picking out the collar which the washer-woman has punished least and your favourite tie, you lay your best suit carefully on the bed. Then having completed as many preparations as possible, you con the situation, reading the letter through and through until you know it by rote and speculating on your chances.

What business is the firm in? Will you get the place? What will they ask you? What manner of man is Mr. X.? These and a score of other questions put themselves to you, and you mentally go through the answers you will give, re-tasting them to see if they are all right.

Well, the day draws its slow length along, and four o'clock finds you on the threshold of the office, dressed as if all the wealth of Midas were at your disposal.

As a matter of fact, you took a single to the City, intending to walk home. With fearsome forebodings of the catechism to come, you pass through the gloomy portals. You notice that there is no inscription over the door, as there was over that other place where Virgil took Dante!

A perky office boy shoves aside the window labelled "Inquiries," and pokes his head through. You ask for Mr. X. "Any appointment?" asks the youth, and you hand him your letter. Presently the lubricated head pops through the aperture again, and jerks out "Ten minutes" in a tone that implies he doesn't think much of your chances, and you register a mental vow that, should you get the job, you will take the first opportunity of clumping his greasy head.

In the small square, box-like room where you sit little of the office can be seen. Rows of dusty filing cases line the walls, and through the "Inquiry" hole you can just see the brass knobs of the copying-press. During the ten minutes you have to wait you survey your record, past life, qualifications, chances of the place, etc., and it is with mingled feelings that you enter the private sanctum.

You are requested to take a seat, and accordingly perch yourself on the extreme edge of a horse-hair covered chair, and gracefully swing your hat between your knees, endeavouring, with small success, to look unconcerned or at least self-possessed.

Then commences the Ordeal.

Where were you last? Um! What did you do there? Um! Why did you leave? Um! No other reason? Um! Understand foreign exchanges? Um! You do the proffered calculation, lires 6103.25 at 25.12, and could swear that through sheer fright it is wrong in about four places.

Have you any references with you? You hand them over. Um! Living with your parents? Um!

Now, why in the name of all that's wonderful do prospective employers invariably ask one that? Is it because you might abscond, and they would then find you better?

What salary did you get? What are you asking now? Um! Well, he has several others to see, and when this is done he will let you know.

Oh! the scores of times you have heard that "let you know"; the scores of times you, hearing it, have hoped against hope; the scores of times they have never let you know. The phrase comes as naturally to your ear as flowers to spring but is not as welcome. Its constant reiteration by various firms has sounded like the passing bell tolling the burial of your hopes in a bottomless pit of despair. "Let you know." Liar!

You get outside, and start the weary walk homewards. You wonder where it will all end. Will he let you know? You doubt it. It is in your bones that he will not. What are your hopes and fears to him? His business is to get the best clerk for the lowest possible salary. He can't afford to let you know you are not wanted. That costs money, and the firm, well, you can guess at their capital. Somewhere about a quarter of a million. You tread in a puddle, and the water oozes through the soles of your boot.

Will he let you know? And if he does, and you get the berth, what does it mean? It simply means that you recommence the same dull routine; nine to six, bill books, ledgers, day-books, all proclaiming to your poverty another man's wealth, and finally, when you are earning the maximum money the firm will pay for your post, the sack (dread word) in favour of a younger and cheaper man.

Taking it altogether, you feel pretty humpy, but the walk livens you up, and by the time home is reached you take a more hopeful view of things. After all, there may be a chance, you may get the job, and anyway, why worry? *Dum spiro, spero!*

But as the postman comes, goes, comes again and goes again, and still you hear nothing, you ask yourself, "Will he ever 'let you know'? Will anyone ever 'let you know'?"

The "Last Workmen's"

Old Saws, Modern Instances.

The maxim maker who is responsible for that well-worn proverb about early rising did not have to catch the "last workmen's." He probably had his breakfast in bed and spent the chilly forenoons between the blankets, philosophising and saw-making.

To get up at half-past six on a bright frosty Sunday morning, and go for a brisk walk along the hard road, this is easy because you are not obliged to do it; but to get up on Monday morning at seven and catch the "last workmen's" calls for effort.

Our watch hangs on the bedpost, and as we wake points to five minutes to seven. Still five minutes in bed. We cuddle down in the warm sheets, and making a splendid resolution to get up as soon as the five minutes are up relapse into that blissful, half-conscious state hovering on the borderland 'twixt sleeping and waking; that semi-oblivion described by Lamb as "chewing the cud of a foregone vision."

Seven strikes. Ugh! It does look cold out of bed. We know it's cold; we are sure of it. While ruminating over the coldness of it we doze and doze, and slip and slide, slowly, beautifully, softly into that dreamy forgetfulness and nearly, very nearly, go to sleep again.

Then our faculties come back with a rush. Twenty past seven! We must, we will get up; but it is so warm here. Oh! for a thick, thick fog that our train may be late.

No, we will not be led astray and with tremendous effort we tear ourselves from the warm embrace of the sheets. Washing and dressing take about twelve and a half minutes. Breakfast about seven and a half, the cocoa cup held with one hand while the other endeavours with indifferent success to button the waistcoat. A quarter to eight sees us in the street.

The "last workmen's" goes at 7.55, and the station is about 18 minutes' walk. We pick up our feet and run; run, even as Jehu the son of Nimshi drove, furiously. Puddles are leaped, roads crossed and traffic threaded with our life balanced on our very eyebrows. Records are made, broken, remade and rebroken. Swiftly we run, for does not our job depend on it, and the "last workmen's" waits for no man.

At length the station. A long queue is dragging its tortuous length before the booking window. More adventurous spirits wrestle with the automatic ticket machine. Amid cries of "Hurry up, please," we get our ticket, and nearly killing the collector in our haste, ascend with painful pantings the horrible staircase. Arrived on the platform we find we have a whole minute to spare.

Here is a striving, struggling crowd, pushing, pulling, plunging to get near the edge. The talk is incessant, but mostly feminine. And as we pass, snatches of conversation dribble into our ears. "So I sez to him, I sez—" "Did you see 'er 'at?" "No! I'm goin' to get some white tulle and make a—" "Yes, and it was 'leven o'clock, and mother says, 'Where've you bin?' "

The clatter and chatter go on, mingling with the stamping of feet, rustling of newspapers being folded, when through it all there cuts a clarion voice, "Brrroo-ad-st. trine. Stand back there."

With a snort and a groan the "last workmen's" pulls up, and then begins a scene which vies with the old gallery door fights at the "Surrey."

The doors fly open and a surging mass of humanity hurls itself at the apertures.

Someone cries "Buck-up, 'Spurs!" but no one has time to laugh.

"Shove" is the order of the day and the 8.15 take the hindermost.

And the Americans say we cannot hustle!

Why, here is the very essence of the strenuous life. If you are going to catch the "last workmen's" you've got to get a move on you—or get left.

We are carried, literally carried into a wooden hut graced with the name of carriage. Six aside are seated where five should be. Ten less fortunate stand in our compartment gripping the beam overhead, and each other. *We* are no "straphangers." No such luck. What are they all grumbling at? They have a strap. Do they want a train each? Let them catch the "last workmen's" on our line, and learn to straphang without a strap. Out upon them for discontented grumblers!

The passengers are a heterogeneous horde, for the "last workmen's" is no respecter of persons. It swallows all and sundry.

The smart clerk with his virgin collar and immaculate tie is leaned upon by the horsey youth with grimy "choker" and greasy quiff.

The dainty shopgirl jostles with her shabby sister and the office boy, proud in the possession of his first "bowler," is pained by the knees of the errand boy deep in the deeds of darkness told in some "Penny Blood."

Class distinction has no sway here. Politeness is almost unknown. The man whose foot you mistake for the floor expects no apology. He may do it himself to-morrow. Frail girls and fair women stand and seated men look on and are not ashamed.

Truly the "last workmen's" is a great leveller of mankind. Those who are seated, well, they got their places by dint of push, and they mean to stick to them.

With those who stand it is a case of what I have I hold, and it has to be held tight, too, or over you go, sideways. However, you can't fall far; there isn't room.

At each successive station the density of the crowd is increased. For every two who alight three or four get in. Moving is out of the question. Reading is an absolute impossibility. Of talk there is little. The men are for the most part surly. The boys discuss their favourite football team, and the girls giggle and tell each other what they said to him and what he said to them, and who was there and what she wore.

At our journey's end the whole original scene is repeated backwards. The train, gorged to repletion with humanity, voids us onto the station just as we were swallowed at the start. The same scamper past the ticket collector, the same hurrying down the stairs until at the station gates we are split into many hurrying streams, all flowing their several ways to swell the ever-growing throng of servitude.

And in the terminus, the "last workmen's," empty as the back of our hand, rests panting from its labours, with never a thought for those it has left behind.

The Staff Dinner

Messrs. Goodbody, Ishmael, and Goodbody having decided that their clerks and other employees should have at least one square meal during the year, a committee was accordingly chosen to arrange the details, the after dinner entertainment, printing of programs, etc. This committee consisted of Bywell, the cashier, Macgregor, the "drummer" (a good judge of whisky was Mac!), Bamford, of the counting-house, and Cross, the shipping clerk.

On the Monday morning we were each given a pink invitation-card announcing that Messrs. Goodbody, Ishmael, and Goodbody would give their First Annual Dinner on the following Friday in the "White Room" at the Jordan Hotel.

In the counting-house that morning little work was done. With ledgers and bill-books ostentatiously open, we discussed and dissected the menu and program.

It became evident that each and every individual who was contributing to the concert had been put down to sing at precisely the most inconvenient time.

Taylor, who was down to sing first, protested on the grounds that vocal exercise immediately after dinner was bad for one; whereat Thompson opined that vocal exercise by Taylor was bad at any time. Anderson, who was to appear last, protested that he absolutely could not sing in a room full of smoke. Webell, who was down for an imitation of farmyard stock and other musical instruments, objected to being put immediately after Taylor, who was sure to empty the room. But these and other suggestions and objections were calmly ignored by the committee, who remained quite confident that "it would all come right on the night."

By special permission, we left our ledgers and invoices an hour earlier than usual on the Friday to allow us time in which to prepare for the banquet. So, punctually at five o'clock, there was a general stampede. The private office looked like nothing so much as the banks of the Serpentine at seven o'clock on a summer's morning. Here were congregated the seniors in varying stages of undress, hastily disrobing to don their camphor-scented and, in many cases, antique, dress-suits.

Downstairs at the wash-bowls there was pandemonium. Here the juniors, who, having no dress-suits, relied solely on a white tie and clean collar to impart a festive appearance to their persons were busily washing, fighting, hair-brushing, and boot-polishing—another person's towel often coming in handy for this last operation.

At a quarter to seven we were at the hotel, where Messrs. Goodbody and Ishmael were assembled, and with these gentlemen we sheepishly exchanged a clammy handshake, as if we now met them for the first time. In one corner of the reception-room a knot of juniors stood anxiously discussing the proper method of eating whitebait, and the best place to put one's table-napkin.

At last the dinner-hour arrived, and found us at table, endeavouring to convince our neighbours that we were thoroughly used to this sort of thing, and awaiting the signal to begin.

A subdued titter went round when it became known that Greig had helped himself to a plateful of olives and was trying to eat them. The warehouseman, also, was heard to remark when the whitebait came round that he "didn't want no silly tiddler-brats. Give him something to eat." But the dinner passed off satisfactorily, and, with little sighs of content, we pushed our chairs away from the table and awaited the usual "Gentlemen, you may smoke."

Then, leaning back with easy grace, and smoking big cigars as if to the manner born, we criticised with freedom and fluency the various items of the entertainment, joined in the usual loyal toasts, and waited for the "boss's" reply to "The Firm."

Mr. Ishmael arose amidst "prolonged applause," as the papers generally put it. It pleased him to see such amicableness between master and man—(was he not paying for the spread?)—he thought the relations between employer and employee should be of a more friendly nature than was usual. (Frantic "Hear, hear!" from Thompson, who was under notice.) He was glad to be able to say that the firm was doing a much better trade than had previously been the case—(twenty-seven mental resolutions were here made to apply for a rise next week)—but big business did not necessarily mean big profits—they had had large expenses, and, notwithstanding a big turnover, could not but anticipate a small profit (the twenty-seven resolutions were here withdrawn). He wound up by expressing a hope that the staff would show its gratitude for the firm's kindness in thus meeting them on an equal footing by increased attention to their duties.

Thompson was here heard to say something about the "tea money" being cut down to sixpence, but the bulk of his remark was lost in the volley of table-rapping following the conclusion of the speech.

The vice now proposed "Our Senior," Mr. Ishmael, than whom he knew no better master or friend. Had he been any other man than himself, he must have blushed like the maiden of bashful fifteen. Of course, we all heartily agreed, signifying the same in the usual manner.

Then, with an occasional thought of the times "our beloved senior" had rowed us, threatened us with the sack, and sacked us, we sang with infinite gusto that time-honoured refrain, "For he's a jolly good fellow." Oh! the snobbery of it!

Every toaster was sure that the person he proposed was the best man breathing, and the toasted was quite convinced that the next man was a better than he, until each successive toast pushed someone further up the ladder of virtue, and every man seemed to be qualifying for a halo.

At eleven o'clock we broke up, some to go home, the more convivial spirits to adjourn to the "Spotted Boar," with the avowed intention, as Withers put it, "of doing it up red."

The next morning saw these "bloods" arrive at the office, somewhat dishevelled in appearance, and with a "morning-after-the-night-before" look on their faces.

But Mr. Ishmael, "our beloved senior," was there, bright and early, carefully noticing how many minutes past nine we each of us arrived.

The Wandering Minstrels

"Peradventure, the gentlemen would like some music to while away the tedious journey. Come in, 'Ector!"

A little fat man with a twinkling and watery eye, and a general air of very much broken-down respectability about his clothes, he carried under his arm a time-worn fiddle, which looked, if possible, a trifle more dilapidated than its owner.

Hector, his colleague, was long and angular. His very life blood must have been acetic acid, so sour and sharp did he look. He was accompanied by a guitar, suspended round his shoulders by a leather bootlace. They entered the third-class carriage and seated themselves opposite each other just as the train started.

"We are not blind, gentlemen," pursued the fiddler, "nor we ain't unemployed. Likewise, we 'ave no starving wives or families. At least, I haven't; but 'Ector—" He thoughtfully left the inference to be drawn.

"We rely solely on our talents for our livin', having no physical imperfections, paralysis, or such to command your sympathy. We're no Marie Halls nor no Kubeliks. We don't want no limelight nor no swagger 'air cut. Have you the rosin, 'Ector? Thank you!"

During this discourse Hector had been indulging in a series of arpeggio twangs on his instrument. Now he lit the stump of a cigarette which had been concealed pen-wise behind his ear. The violinist went on:

"This instrument I am about to edify you with is a real, a genuwine 'Armarti,' made specially for me by that gentleman. My partner in the musical business is directly descended from a well-known family, having been disinherited by a stern parent for comin' home late at night."

26

Here the fallen scion of a noble house suggested that the speaker should "cut the cackle"; and as the audience showed some signs of impatience, the concert began.

"By your leave, gentlemen, we will commence our Horatio with the well-known 'Moonlight Sonata.' 'Ector, strike the lyre."

A wavering screech from the fiddle, as of a soul in distress, a tinkle from the guitar, and there follows a mournful wailing. To this jigging arrangement both performers kept time, such as it was, with their heads and feet. Presently the strains of the fiddle became more painful, more yearning, and with a heartrending howl, the duet came to an end.

"There you are, gents! You might pay five bob for a seat somewhere to hear a bloke with yards of shirt-front do that, and not do it half so well either, mind you. But such is life! True talent is never recognised. My friend opposite will now oblige with a song. I might add, gentlemen, that, between you and me, there's only one thing keeps 'Ector off the operatic stage, and that is, 'e can't get fat, and they won't 'ave thin 'uns. Proceed, 'Ector!"

So Hector tells his audience, in a voice like iron filings, that " 'e wants ter see the dear old 'ome ergain; ter sit once more beside the cottage foire"—the while his partner takes up the collection, his comments thereon being a mixture of intense gratitude and withering sarcasm.

"Thank you, sir! Here's a real gentleman as appreciates talent, and signifies the same in the usual manner ... May I ask you to contribute? No? P'raps I've come at a bad time. Possibly the gentleman has left his small silver in his other trousis. Sorry I can't change a fiver, dear boy ... No, we don't take coppers. We snatches 'em. If you give me your card, I'll call to-morrow, when perchance your missus could sell the bones and raise the necessary. Time's no object where money's concerned. Well, I won't worry the gentleman. No ear for music, perhaps? Well, well; we can't all be Pierpont Morgins ... Thank *you*, sir. I could see it in your eye. You fairly bubbles over with generosity. Your givin' bump must be very big, I'm sure.

"... 'Ave you all done, gentlemen? No more superfluous cash knocking around? Very good! ... 'Ector, I have much pleasure in informing you that we have the magnificent sum of threepence halfpenny." The guitar stopped. "What do you suggest? Shall we winter at Mentone or doss out? Perhaps you'd like to build a few libraries. I've had my eye on a lovely Pan'ard motor, all painted red; but on second thoughts, I think I shall indulge in a mild and bitter.

"Well, gentlemen, you needn't worry about us. We don't do this for a livin'. Being both independent gentlemen, with large fortunes, we seeks to kill time by doing good for others. Our next performance takes place in the adjoining carriage. Admission by ticket only, to be obtained at the bookin' office or of the usual agents. There is no limit to what you gives.

"Good-night, gentlemen! Follow me, 'Ector, and mind the step."

Then on the platform—"Perish me pink! Thruppence 'a'penny. And our fare was fourpence."

A Night Out

There were two of us—and the moon.

We started at five o'clock from the South side of London, and knew not where we were going. Nor for that matter did we care, so long as we left streets and houses behind us.

It was cold, cold as Charity, and there were the dregs of a snowfall about. In half an hour we saw our last electric tram.

In an hour we were traversing a long, straight road, devoid of lamps, pavements, houses, devoid of everything but ourselves and the moonlight. We looked about us. Nothing but the cold earth wrapped in its surplice of snow, a bit threadbare in places, but very beautiful under the moon. Night itself seemed frozen hard, and nothing moved.

After about three miles of this, with the deadly silence growing upon us, broken only by the crunch of the frozen road under our feet and the purr of our pipes, we felt that to keep silence longer would be unbearable. So we sang. We lifted up our voices in anything that would go with a swing. Now it was "Simon the Cellarer," now half-remembered snatches of "Hiawatha," songs of "Chibiabos," and again some roaring drinking song. And our voices filled the firmament, coming back to us in belated echoes from the woods, yea, from the moon and her dark blue back-cloth.

How many lonely cottagers we scared, how many steaming, sleeping cows we disturbed we knew not. And cared not so long as we sang.

We must have walked eight to ten miles in this fashion. Where to we knew not, except that the moon, like—well, like nothing else in nature and most unlike the moon of London, was always on our left. And, of course, there was the Plough, with the help of which one can always find the North Star. And nothing came along to tell us where we were. There was no life but us. We might have been dropped on some burnt-out, frozen other world.

Then a signpost. It took 28 matches to read that signpost. We counted them. And then it was unreadable. But on its post we found a bill, and by the moon's light we read it. It told of a sale of farm stock, amongst which was a foal.

"Out of 'Gris Chunder,' by"—by what do you think? By Chibiabos! And again we lifted up our voices.

> Sing to us, O Chibiabos,
> Songs of love and songs of longing.

Then we looked at the address of the auctioneer, and looked at one another in amaze. Where were we? Was he a local man? Had we really come so far? How should we get back? Finally we decided that if we kept on we should certainly get somewhere. Brighton perhaps.

So at a good swinging four to the hour we went on and on and still on, with the moon on our left, the Plough behind and Orion with his Belt in front. And we thought of people, hordes of people sitting in stuffy theatre galleries, and we congratulated ourselves. What superior beings we were! We trespassed into a hedge, and a frightened thrush came out with a fearful clatter and a sound of tearing silk, and flew with a "cluck-cluck" across the road. And further on, as we turned a sharp corner, something rose from our path and fled away with a whirr of wings into the night, back to the dark Plutonian shore.

When we had nearly walked to the ends of the earth we thought of things earthly again, amongst which were times and trains and home. Half-past nine. Another mile, and we saw a light through the trees, the first for hours. We arrived at the cottage, and a penny decided which of us should knock. After repeated rappings and a magic row of shadow-shapes across the blind, a timorous voice asked who was there. We asked where we were, and we could hear the poor woman tremble. Then from behind the door came directions. Turn to the right, and about four miles would bring us to a village. We thanked the voice and withdrew. We did two miles of the four, and then found a signpost. We also found that the voice had mistaken left for right, and we had, perforce, to do the two sides of a triangle, which we soon proved without the aid of Euclid were greater than the third side. Then the road broadened, and an inn came in sight. It was the Pike and Anchor, whose beer was nectar.

We borrowed an antediluvian timetable and a hunk of bread and cheese. Nearest station, four miles; time, 10.15; last train for London, 10.43. Four miles in 28 minutes, and Charing-cross 20 miles away. Of course, we couldn't do it; but we started.

Half a mile had been done when we heard wheels. Behind us, too, and coming our way. A private omnibus—but full up inside and out with people and luggage. Were they going for the 10.43? Yes, and there was a strap and a door handle. We took one each, and ran.

How we ran! Ran until we forgot we had legs, and only knew that we had two long aches where our legs had been. A man in the carriage inquired after my second wind. I spluttered and spat and gasped. Another said he was cold. We were not! And as we contorted our faces they in the carriage smiled and cheered us on. But we wanted no goad but thoughts of home and supper. For our bread and cheese was far behind, in the Pike and Anchor.

We had run about 3,000 Irish miles and some odd furlongs when we saw the station. Then we breathed, painfully at first. Two minutes to spare, and those who had been in the bus stamped their feet, while we wiped our brows.

In the train we looked at one another and smiled. We could have grinned at death, then. On the opposite seat lay a man who cursed the train for a creeping thing and beat his fingers and wrapped his body in a blanket. And we wiped our foreheads and smiled.

At home we ate cold beef and pickles and cheese and bread, and smoked and smiled and went to bed, and slept and slept and slept. Next day we could hear our joints creak as we limped along, and we smiled. For we had had eight hours of life, real life, for three shillings.

A Winter Foreword

I sat at my window, and thoughtfully bit at my pencil, searching in vain for the inspiration that would not come. Down in the garden a plump starling was playing tug-of-war with a worm which evidently objected to being dragged from its bed in the lawn.

Summer had gone, and winter was knocking at the door with little cold taps. Presently he would begin to kick and thump, then to buffet and batter, until at last he gained entry. But to-day the sky was blue, and little woolly flecks of cloud were running races across it. It was not a day for work, so I bit my pencil. Then it was that the gate clicked and creaked, and a voice with all the joy of life in it sang:

> It was a lover and his lass.

Now, this is essentially a duet, so I took the stairs three at a time, and found Helen in the garden. I pointed out to her that she had spoiled my day's work.

"Work?" she said. "Come out for a walk. Look at the weather and—look at me."

I looked—and fell. Inwardly marvelling at my lack of will, I went indoors to get a stick and some more tobacco. There would be many, many wet and dreary days on which to work, I told myself; and got much comfort from the reflection.

> Now, therefore take the present time,
> > With a hey! and a ho! and a hey nonino!

sang Helen.

Inside half an hour we were in the forest. And such a forest! I raced Helen down a glade and up the slope, and there we stopped, panting, to look around us. It is bitterly cold, and our breath comes frostily, but the blood tingles and sings through our veins with a new-found ardour. We move boot-deep through a sea of red-hot beech leaves, from which the green boles of the oaks rise gaunt and bare, like weed-covered derelicts, their bent and broken masts leaning all ways. Autumn is bidding us adieu, and gathering up her faded and bedraggled skirts dances her fitful dance through the woods as if she were yet young and sprightly.

In a thorn-bush by the pond a robin perches, tuning up against the dark days, when he shall be the only thing left to gladden our hearts with sweet-toned promises of the spring to come. There is one little cadenza he is not quite sure of, and again and again he tries it over until it is perfect. Then he flies away to get his feathers ready for the full-dress rehearsal. Here and there through the drifted beech leaves rise little round-topped toadstools, pink and white, as the skin of a babe. At these, Helen tells me, the fairies will sup from acorn cups when we are gone.

Down the hill we go, scattering the leaves and scaring every living thing with our haste. At the foot of the hill is a cemetery, a giant's graveyard; a graveyard of fallen trees and rotted stumps, with moss as their only epitaph; a veritable valley of dry bones. Above, in a tall elm, a wood-pigeon makes warm little cooings, bubbling and crooning like a mother to her child. Little else is to be heard but the snap of twigs beneath our feet and the swish of Helen's skirts as she goes breast-high through the bracken, which springs from the earth and waves in the wind like pale flames; the still unquenched fires of summer. The blackberry bushes and briers, with a few torn and scarred leaves listlessly clinging to them, are here and there brightened by a deserted spider's-web, all be-jewelled with hoarfrost. These, Helen tells me, are the hammocks which Peas-blossom and Mustard-seed have woven for Titania and her train.

Now we wander through a stately cathedral, whose pillars are lordly elms, and whose altar-cloth is the green ivy, its roof the sky. Presently comes a clearing in the wood, and from the friendly shelter of a gaudy holly tree we watch half a dozen rabbits frisking and sporting on the green; now backing and dodging, now jumping and twisting in the intricacies of some corner game. This second edition of summer has got into their blood. I strike my stick smartly on the tree trunk, and before ever the echo has re-echoed from the wood there is never a rabbit in sight.

A wisp of the north wind comes across the open, and begins in its kittenish way to frolic and sport with an old and lusty oak, who slowly and sagely nods his hoary head as who would say, "Aha! But it will take a lot of that to hurt me." "Possibly," whispers the wind, "but you must understand I am only just stretching myself. Wait until this little kitten has grown into the full-limbed tiger; wait until January, when I shall have come into my strength and power. Then I will play with you." And with a derisive giggle it flirts away to tease the reeds fringing the half-frozen pond. I wanted to write poetry all this time, but found my thoughts would not materialise.

We sat on a natural seat formed by a crippled and distorted willow, and watched a merry squirrel swinging along one of his tree highways, jumping from branch to branch, swinging here, running there, sure-footed, and entirely wonderful. The rooks are busy, too, if noise be their business. For they fight and flap about the tree-tops, sweeping and making ample curves through the blue and white of the sky.

But the shadows have now merged into the general darkness, and the mists of night are falling. The hollows and dips are already filled with ghostly vapours, and the sun has gone—no, not yet gone. For, on emerging from the wood, we find the gates of the western sky all afire, and it is like the blare of many trumpets. It is as if there were mutiny in heaven, and the wrath of ages is being poured out upon the earth. It lights and scorches the pale birchen twigs, and a majestical beech which has not yet shed all its rags, catches the glint, and breaks into wisps of golden fire, beautiful against the black of the wood beyond.

And so home. Down the deep cut lane, where a few starlings are still foraging, and through whose hedges comes the tired bleat and cough of the sheep. Then Night, the "sober suited matron all in black," lays her heavy hand on all, while one by one the stars are pricked into the heavens.

The Call of the Downs

It was one bright morning last week when I first found out that I was very ill. On my way to the railway station to miss the eight-thirty for the City I have to pass through a churchyard, a hoary, unkempt churchyard, where in the summer the cold, grey stones are hid in a riot of rank grass and weeds, and round whose edge a regiment of elms keeps watch over the sleepers. In one sheltered corner a cracked and weather-beaten stone leans awry, and on this one may read that "Here Lyeth Amos Bennett, Gentleman, who planted the trees in this churchyard."

Many a morning when those trees, forgetting their duty as watchers of the dead, have danced and clapped their hands to the song of the wind, I also have lifted up my voice in praise and thanks to Amos Bennett.

On this particular morning I was late in leaving home; and accordingly on reaching the churchyard I leaned over the railings while I filled my pipe and mused on the absurdity of work and the beauties of a cluster of gummy chestnut buds. Over against the tram stables a thrush broke into song. "Queen, my queen," he said. "A-little-bit-of-bread-and-no-cheeeeese!" And from the rectory garden his mate answered with a light and amorous, "Cheer up, cheer up, chuck!"

That was really the beginning of things. I wandered slowly on my way, thinking of green pastures and still waters, of sea-scented breezes and blossom starred hedges, with the sheep tearing the grass on the shady side. Then the eight-thirty rumbled over the bridge, and was lost to me for ever. So I caught the eight-forty-five. And so I am sick. Sick for the smell of the sea-weed on the foreshore, for the sting of the spray, for the salt on my eyelids and the wind in my face. I want to climb the Downs, toiling up from the landward side; to stand on the highest point with the Channel spread below me; to bare my head to the southerly wind and fill my lungs to the brim with long draughts of sweet air. There is a little grass-clad shelf of cliff too, where I would again lie and peer over on to the rocks below, watching the gulls sweeping and screaming beneath me, and listening to the dull, comforting murmurs of the waves on the beach.

Work has been a farce these five days. I find myself staring out of the window at nothing, whilst in my mind's eye I see the warm breezes rippling across the tops of the corn, and watch the shadows of the clouds as they sweep down the meadow land. And the joy of the dark pines against the blue, or the moon filtering through the lacework of a silver birch!

Going home I sit in the train trying to read my evening paper. It falls on my knees and I stare out of the window with eyes that see only the geometrical precision of the hop poles of Kent as they march fanwise beside me. When will that holiday list come out? When am I to have my fortnight's freedom? I want to lie on my back and stare and stare up through the trees into the sky, and sing and shout with the wind and race with the waves.

In a time like this there is solace in a time table, and last night I spent two pleasant hours with a Bradshaw, revisiting the glimpses of the sun. And what joy there is in a road map! Here are Surrey and Sussex spread beneath me, and again I am plodding along the hard white road which will lead me to the sea. Always the sea!

Yesterday I walked down the Embankment to listen to the lap, lap of the muddy water as it smacked against the prisoning walls. There was music in the hooting of a tug; for it reminded me of those soft evenings spent on the beach with Her, when we heard the warning syrens and saw the sparkle of the gallant ships as they sped away into the dusk; when we watched the flaming sword of Cape Grisnez sweep the sky and return to its scabbard. The Embankment has a strange fascination for me. For there you may see more sky at a glance than anywhere else in London.

What do you town dwellers know of the sky, the ceaseless pageantry of its clouds, its wonderful colours, its merry fits, its sulky moods, its fearful anger? You walk about, buried in bricks and mortar, seeing only a long narrow strip of smoke-stained heaven between the roofs, and that only when you wonder if it will rain. Come with me and see the sky from the top of the South Downs, where the clouds sail across the blue, darkening the sea and land; where it stretches before you and behind in one vast blue dome, limitless and incomprehensible. Or see it torn by wintry gales, when the wind roars in your ears and blows your hair upright; when the frightened clouds stampede and the maddened sea horses are lashed into impotent fury.

So now you know why I am ill. This sickness came upon me last year, but owing to the bad weather it was a little later. Then I cured it with an ordnance map, a ground ash stick, an old briar pipe, and a pocket edition of Keats. With these I tramped southwards to the sea. I remember one day, after doing fifteen miles, stopping, hot and tired, to bathe my feet in a cool, willow-shielded brook, which giggled and danced over my grateful toes while I smoked and read.

> To one who has been long in city pent,
>   'Tis very sweet to look into the fair
> And open face of Heaven—to breathe a prayer,
>   Full in the smile of the blue firmament.

I shall not be better until I have done it all over again. Every little reminder of freedom which I see stings me and makes my longing deeper. A railway poster, a steamship advertisement, a chance phrase in a book will conjure up memories of past holidays, and the more I chafe the more the shackles cut into me. A night or two ago I lay abed glancing through a volume of Richard Jefferies. Two chapters I read; and then I put the book away to lean out of the window and watch the stars running away from the morning. The poor, starved tree beneath my window waved and whispered in the wind; and I thought I could once more hear the surge of the waves as they broke and ran, dragging the shrieking pebbles after them. Now I know why boys run away to sea, or endeavour to emulate Capt. Kidd or Ned Kelly. I shall run away presently; and when I am posted missing you may lay the blame on two thrushes in a churchyard and one Amos Bennett, Gentleman.

A Night Awake

Within half an hour of going to bed I came to the conclusion that I was not to sleep. I tried the many charms and incantations prescribed for me at various times by friends who always sleep well, but, as usual, they failed me. I counted sheep passing through a gateway until the whole flock broke and ran; I watched waving corn until the bed went round and round; I repeated the numbers up to one hundred and then stopped, because I could not think what came after one hundred and eight.

Then I gave it up. Turning over, I punched the pillow into some semblance of comfort, and turned it for the fifth time to get the cool side, only to find it still warm. I wandered round the room in the dark to find matches, but did not stub my toe against the table, because I have wandered round the room in the dark before, many times, and I am beginning to know the way. I found tobacco, pipe and matches, and climbed into bed again. There was light enough to smoke by, although it was but two o'clock. The sky was ashen grey, paler in the east, where, behind the houses, the moon had started on her long journey.

So I doubled my pillow; and, wrapping the bedclothes around me like a Red Indian, sat up, disconsolate, to wait for the morning. Through the long hours I sat there in a silence broken only by the occasional bark of a dog and the purr of my pipe.

As the moon went down, the sky got paler and a cock crew. An answering call came from a little way away; and faintly in the distance another told the sleeping world that he, too, was awake. For some minutes these three tossed the talk about, until, one missing his turn, the conversation languished.

Then suddenly, as if at a word of command, the edges of the little watery clouds blushed pink, and a shudder seemed to pass through the earth. Day had come; fresh and bright-eyed day. On the leaden gutter opposite a sparrow appeared, rubbed a fist into each tired eye, pecked his shirt-front into shape, passed his beak carefully down each wing, and said, "Pip, pip."

The lady from the fourth tile came next. She bustled out of her front door, patted her back hair, and then turned to bellow up the passage to her lie-a-bed spouse. Then she flew off to have her morning dip in a puddle somewhere, and by this time the whole row of cottages was awake and chattering like a sewing circle.

"Yes, me dear. He came home in a shockin' state. Wonder he didn't wake the street. I had such a job with him!"

"Ah, she's no better than she should be, not a bit! Carries herself so high, too. Bold as brass! Hussy, that's what she is!"

The lady mentioned overheard, and lifting her head a trifle higher, sniffed and murmured, "Person!"

"Person, indeed!" spluttered the first. "And me with sons out and doing well. Person, indeed."

And now they are at it. The business of the day has begun. Husbands and fathers become embroiled, children scream at the doors, feathers are pulled, and as the quarrel dwindles, the harassed husbands retire to the chimney-stack to pull their collars straight and apologise to each other.

"You understand, old chap! Yes, of course! Must do it. Old woman never let me rest if I didn't. Sorry about your eye though. Let's go over to the cab rank. There's some good oats there."

And away they fly, followed by the threatening screams of their wives. They are very like human beings, these sparrows. See the proud mothers showing off their children or gossiping at the doors, apron over arm. Here young Romeo comes wooing, until he espies old man Capulet limping round the corner, bedraggled and gouty. He was out late last night, and looks it.

The women folk are busy now, hearth-stoning the doorsteps, or getting the youngsters ready for school.

"Keep still, I tell you! How do you think I can put your feathers straight if you keep wriggling about like that … Now off you go, and you come home with as much as a single spot on your pinny, and see what I'll give you. Yes, as you say, mum! It's a terrible job keeping 'em tidy. Send 'em out in the morning as clean as a new pin, and I'll be bound they come home as black as tinkers!" And the good lady bustles indoors to get ready for her spouse, who has promised to come home early with a load of straw and do the front room out.

At the end of the row the village butcher has his stall. I know he is the butcher, because for the last half hour he has done nothing but shout out "Arf a leg. Arf a shoulder. Cheap, cheap, cheap!" Presently, along the wall below, creeps a fiendish tortoiseshell cat. Warily she goes, for the wall is topped with broken glass. Every yard or so she stops and looks meaningly at the roof, but she knows that it is out of her reach. And so do the sparrows; for they sit along the gutter in a grinning row, and put out their tongues, while here and there a younger one will put his thumb unto his nose and spread his fingers out.

And so the comedy goes on, until the clock next door strikes six, when I lay my pipe aside and snuggle down into the bed to try to snatch a few minutes sleep from the fast retreating night. But a tenor-robusto milkman is chanting his war-song down the road; so I get up.

Later, my friends at the railway station look at my weary eyes and say, "Hullo. Where did you get to last night? You look pretty rotten." Which is precisely how I feel.

The River

"O-old Uncle Tom Cobleigh, and all." The door of the "Fish and Eels" slammed behind us and cut off the end of the long-drawn line. This hostelry stands by the river; and, inside, a rowing club was holding a triumph. But by nine o'clock the atmosphere of the taproom was nearly opaque, and so we two stepped out for some air. Standing on the wooden bridge across the weir, we looked down to where the moon's reflection lay split into wriggling shreds of pale flame on the torn and twisted water. The night was soft and sweet, and as the shouting behind us ceased, and the pipes and tankards finished their tattoo on the tables, we listened to the gentle lapping of the water against the stonework of the bridge and the sleepy sighing of the light winds in the tree-tops. Before us lay the river, silvery and cool; behind us the falling stream made most excellent music; and so we decided to walk home.

There are few things more peaceful than a river by night. The caressing murmur of the little wavelets as they break over the pebbles; the trickle of an unseen spring paying its tribute to the mother river; the whisper of the rushes as they bend and nod in the swirl of a backwater; all these sounds make the deep silence deeper yet. The melancholy talking of the hurrying waters as they flow onwards to the far-away sea, through pleasant valleys fat with young corn, past flower-entwined cottage and smoky factory, through chattering village and roaring town, breeds in the mind a healing quiet, and in the darkness of night this grows upon one until conversation becomes a superfluity. Another mile, and then a gate, on which we rested. It seemed a sin to strike matches and so break the charm of that wonderful night.

Above, the stars burned on their courses, and the moon, pale with watching, shed her glory over the earth. A splash in the water told where a rat had dived, and the quivering circles widened and widened until lost in the opposite bank.

Silence, black, velvety silence, and the smothered laughter of the river. Then, like a streak of light, a nightingale began to sing. Rising and falling in a shower of glorious harmony, swelling and dwindling in an ecstasy of burning passion, the trembling love song pierced the night, now merrily dancing, light as a rose-petal on a fountain, now throbbing with pent-up agony and pleading. Sometimes it seemed as if, prisoned within the bird, a soul was striving to make itself understood, to explain the charm which should set it free.

Again, a wealth of strung melodies tripped across the listening air, and floating upwards, made new stars in heaven. Afraid to move, we sat and listened, and twice I swallowed a lump in my throat. It was Ophelia's death-song in a new setting, a setting of pearly moonlight and star-scattered sky. And when it stopped, it was as if a light had gone out. From the opposite bank the litany was taken up, and once more the sparkling cadenzas leapt into life. The delirious joy of Spring, the ripened love of Summer, the despair of Autumn, and the cold grey death of Winter drifted across the memory on that trembling tide of music. Like falling stars, the plaintive notes lit the night hush with points of fire, and the whole world stood still to listen. For the next half-mile the melody followed us, then slowly died away.

It was quite an hour later that we discovered we were tired and thirsty; and as midnight was long past, our chances of getting relief were few. So we plodded on, under low-hanging alder trees, through whose branches the moonlight fell fretted on the ground; now past bushes round which the air hung heavy with scent; by orchards, where the white-washed tree-trunks shone like the ghosts of an army. Presently through the half-light loomed the figure of a man, and we heard his dolorous whistle as he dragged a tow-rope across the path to where, in the hedge, an old white horse stood patiently munching. We struck a bargain, and dropped over the coping of the lock to a load of warm bricks. Here was rest indeed, and with the help of a sack of fodder and a coil of rope we improvised a fairly comfortable couch.

From the mousehole of a cabin the steersman rose like a stage devil, and when I licked my parched lips, sank again to return with a stone bottle of water, which gurgled into the tin cup as if impatient to be drunk.

Eastwards the dome above us was now warm with rosy light, and a few tiny flecks of cloud swam in the sky like wind-blown May blossom. One frozen spark alone showed where the last star lay on its lilac bed, nigh unto death. A lark woke in a field and went up to sing his morning hymn. But we had heard the nightingale! Once a grave old horse put his head over the hedge and whinnied, and heavy cattle stood knee-deep in the reeds, staring round-eyed at us, or clambered awkwardly up the bank from their morning drink.

As the day advanced and the sun lit the tops of the distant trees, gaudy dragonflies came out and flashed hither and yon through the maze of water weeds. The morning air, as yet unsullied by contact with the smoke of the town, blew upon us straight from the mountains of its birth. And on its breath there came to us the glamour of the poppy-splashed cornfields, the sweetness of the clover clumps with their drowsy bees and the twang of burning heath and wood smoke.

And thus we moved along, gently, as one drifts into a dream, past golden fields and dew-hung hedges; by little patches of woodland, where Puck might have danced, or Nick Bottom wakened from his most rare vision; and so to where the houses became more frequent, and gradually into the town.

But when once our tired feet touched hard pavements, and our eyes saw the yawning night policeman, all the romance vanished, and there was nothing left for us but home and bed.

Motley

Rosalind had spoken the epilogue; and, as she fluttered through the bushes to her tiring-house, I withdrew to let the crowd which had been watching the pastoral play break up and dwindle until I was alone. A breeze with a faint chill in it stirred the tall grasses, and between the stems of the distant poplars the sky glowed red where day strove hopelessly with night. I pushed my stick into the yielding earth and sat down under a flaming copper beech. A leaf floated to the ground close by, and an inquisitive sparrow dropped to investigate. Then I heard a snatch of song somewhere in the undergrowth before me; the bushes parted, and a man came out.

In the half-light I could not see him distinctly, but as he drew nearer I saw that he wore a long cloak and swung a frond of bracken in his hand. He came directly towards me, and, thinking that he was not aware of my presence, I coughed.

"That's all right," he called cheerily. "I saw you come from yonder, and thought to have a chat. May I sit here?"

He stared at me for some seconds, wrapped his cloak round his legs, and sat down.

"Have the gods made thee poetical?" he asked. "And yet they must have done so, or you would not be sitting here. A glorious sky, is it not? Who am I? Well, half an hour ago I was Touchstone. Three nights agone I took Puck. Very heavy work, Puck! So much hopping, skipping, and jumping. Yet one must live. In a day or two I start work in earnest as Autumn; bluff Autumn in a motley suit of brown and gold."

"But surely," I remonstrated, "Autumn is an old man, or at best but of middle age."

He wrinkled the corners of his eyes.

"Your poets and painters have done this thing," he said. "They paint Spring as a young girl, Summer as a full-blown beauty, Autumn as a man on in years, and Winter always carries a snowy poll. All wrong! All wrong! Now, mark ye! Spring is a well-knit and a lusty youth with nearly all the strength of Winter, but without his vile temper. Summer is a blowsy female, fat and sleepy. You have heard of Audrey? She generally gets the job of Summer. Oh, yes, I married her, but we do not agree well together. She has no more voice than your plain-song cuckoo; and an apt quotation from the classics is as aloes in her mouth.

"I am Autumn, and my mission is to kick you a bit to get you ready for my successor, who is a knave a trifle younger than myself—a giant of knotted limbs and thews of steel with the very devil of a temper. Swaggering Pistol does that, as a rule; and he plays it with a two-handed sword. If he should come a bit before his time, then I have to keep my weather eye open and 'ware shins." He laughed softly and plucked a grass blade.

"Now, that old cynic Jaques said I was a fool. But methinks a fool must needs be a philosopher, and most philosophers are fools, though they know it not. To fool when the wind is searching out the weak parts of one's garments, when one's nose is blue and fingertips dead to all feeling, argues the philosophical mind. But Jaques suffered with his liver:

> A merry heart goes all the day,
> Your sad tires in a mile-a.

"Yes, I've played Autolycus. A blackguard part! A cutpurse rogue! Touchstone's all right, but I shall not weep when the company goes into winter quarters. I rest then. Theatres are far too stuffy. Give me the open heath and the curlew's scream! Next week I begin to rehearse my new part. Over the hills, across the moors, through fen and forest I shall scamper like a spring colt, painting my scenery as I go. The oak shall blush at my coming; the beech flame into gold; while the robin so gay shall tune up his lay, as the sheep tinkle into the fold. I shall hang my lamps in the hedgerows to lighten the snowdrop's way, while the little spring flowers are counting the hours until the earth blossoms to May. And when I am harried by Winter with icy sword and keen, the ivy and holly with berries so jolly shall keep my memory green."

He pulled a dandelion head and blew upon it. "Eight o'clock," he said.

"Jaques said you took a dial from your poke to see the time," I pointed out. "You cannot tell it from a dandelion!"

"You never know," he answered. "It might easily be right. As to the dial, spring's a slack time with us, and so—

"Just now I'm acting as ganger and foreman of works. Nights I'm busy rounding up the Little Folk, Peasblossom and Mustardseed and that crowd; getting in my stocks of dew-pearled cobwebs, hips and haws and mushrooms, and drawing fairy rings in the grass. The swallows will soon want herding, too. Yes, I know it's most of it Puck's work, but he's twisted his ankle trying to break the record in his famous girdling act. Got round the earth in thirty-nine and a few seconds, though he crocked himself doing it. So I'm coupling his odd jobs with mine."

"And how about your women folk?" I inquired.

"Women?" he repeated. "Well, we did have one in to help Spring clear up when Winter had stayed a bit late. She was supposed to sow cowslips and daffy-downdillies, help the young shrubs, and give the silver birches a rub here and there, filling in her spare time opening buds. But, bless your heart, she spent half her days looking at her features in a pool. Lord, what features! Audrey is the only other woman, and she does fairly well at times. But she's a poor thing; an ill-favoured thing!"

A wood pigeon coo-ed in the branches above us, and I shivered. "I like my work," my companion went on, "but I cannot stand the winter. Autumn's the only season! Motley's the only wear! Did you ever sit by the side of a brook and watch the leaves swirling and twisting down from up-country? Beaten copper, burnished bronze, ashy steel, hoary silver and ruddy gold. That's me! When you get up in the morning and see the little hollows in the wood filled with shifting white mist and the chestnut twigs all dripping; when the brown carpet at your feet is bright with dew, and the little pink toadstools are peeping through. That's me! ...

"But I've stayed long enough. You've yawned twice, and I've got a dance on. No, I'm sorry! You cannot come; it's private. Down by the Hollow Pond, where the split oak lies. And Titania will be there. Nice girl, Titania, but a bit of a shrew. Au revoir, then! Next time you see me you'll not know me."

He turned his coat collar up, smiled and nodded curtly; then rustled into the undergrowth.

I took a motor-bus home, and asked the conductor to put me down at the Forest of Arden.

"Don't know it," he said. "D'you mean the Forester's Arms?"

The Pleasures of Hope

A day or two ago I was reading an article in a magazine which concluded with the remark, "And now, good-bye to work for a space, and hey! for the open road."

Now this is distinctly unfair. I have had my holiday, and this person has no right to gloat over me—to flaunt his riches before my eyes. A long, long time ago, nearly two months, I believe, I was on the open road in the time of the honeysuckle and dog-rose; while he is going in the season of cool days, misty twilights, gaudy hedgerows, scarlet hips and haws, and nuts and blackberries. Now my skin has changed from the colour of a ripe filbert to that of an anaemic suet-pudding, and I must wait a whole ten months before I can put on my thick boots again. Ten months! October, November, December (oh, heavens!), January, February, March (alas!), April, May (ah!), June, July, and then—

To tide me over this awful time I have invented a new game. I have reconstructed my holiday from the ruins thereof. Yesterday, as is my custom, I walked along the Embankment to look at the river and watch the gulls cutting figures of eight through the drab sky. And at the end of the river, you know, there is the sea; the sea just as I saw it from Cuckmere when a roaring southwester was tearing its way inland and the grey rags of cloud took fright and scurried to the north.

Crossing Blackfriars-bridge, I came by ways devious to Bankside. Here at places there is no embankment, and one may get quite close to the water. For the most part the beach is loathsome black mud, with tin cans protruding here and there, but at one wharf a load of real pebbles has been deposited, and over these the wash of a tug will tumble and boil in most realistic fashion. It was on Bankside, you will tell me, that the Globe Theatre stood, and against that post Shakespeare may have leaned with the manuscript of the "Winter's Tale" under his arm. But I know better! It was on Bankside that I stood wrapped in a coastguard's oilskins, watching the green waves tearing at the cliffs, and running back, broken and shrieking, to the sea.

Crossing the bridge again, I wander through to the Temple, where, in a little square, a fountain is playing. This, you will say, is where Ruth Pinch would meet John Westlock. Yet listen awhile! The tinkle of the water as it dances merrily in the basin, the quarrelling of the sparrows as they take their bath, the crooning bubble of the pigeons in the trees above—these are pregnant with memories, and if the man with the gold braid round his hat should be at dinner, I may sit on the railings and run these thoughts over in my mind. There was a little echoing wood not far from Ditchling Beacon, through whose gloom a brook ran laughing. That was where I found a half-fledged blue-tit fallen from its nest, and was severely henpecked by its anxious mother when I tried to put it back. There were wood-pigeons, too, to hush me to sleep, and a saucy yellow hammer, who said "Chee, chee!" derisively when my paper boats came to grief on the shallows of the stream.

The next move in my game in across Fleet-st. to Holborn, where in Staple-inn I can sit under the big plane tree, whose brave pennons of red and russet and gold droop in the breeze. Here the roar of the traffic is sunk to a mere twilight of sound, a whisper such as the breakers make when you are lying on the cliffs above. I never sit under that tree but I expect to hear a cock crow or a dog bark, and see mine host, with brown arms akimbo and red flabby cheeks, come through the doorway. One day he will do so, and then I shall order a hunk of bread, a wedge of cheese, and a pint of cider.

Sometimes I go to the Tower Wharf and see the gallant ships in the murky pool; ships with wonderful names on their turtle-backs— *Christiania, Valparaiso, Riga.* Do you remember lolling by the sea one July noon, when the beach quivered in the heat and the ripples just moved? Then it was that those same ships came and went before you, and you listened to the chug, chug of their screws, and lazily wondered whither they were bound, and, wondering, nearly fell asleep. Then you tried to read, but gave that up in favour of filling the sea with pebbles—a task you had not nearly accomplished by tea-time. Do you remember?

But when I am chewing the cud of my foregone visions like this, there are two things which spoil the illusion. First, the smells of London; the twang of petrol fumes and fried fish from a back court, and on hot days the smell of the tar which boils and blisters on our roadways. Never a whiff of that keen salt air which searches out all your nooks and crannies, and in four breaths rebuilds you!

Second, I may not shout. You have seen a plump, healthy baby stripped for its bath, tumbling about in its mother's lap; cramming her apron into its mouth with both fists, and taking it out again to yell— not to cry peevishly, but to yell because it has no clothes on, and it feels good. I have stood on top of the highbrowed cliffs when the gale halloo-ed across the wastes of sea and the tall thistles lay down before it. I have screamed and yelled, and bid the winds blow and crack their cheeks, even as Lear did. Perhaps I was as mad as Lear; perhaps I was like the baby, full of the joy of life which must either out or smother me.

But I may not do these things in London, nor do I want to. There is no reason for them, and there are too many people about. Neither may I run headlong down the sleek green hills, slashing at the nettles with my ground ash. These are the things which one must do alone to do properly.

If you should try your hand at my game, and it is better than dominoes and coffee in your dinner-hour, do not go near a railway station. I went to London-bridge once and watched a train come in from the South. And I thought of the little green oases it had rattled past, of the dark woods it had plunged into, of the roar of the tunnel through the cliff, and the sudden burst of sunlight and blue sea when the train came out, and you let the window down. And I nearly cried!

For, although it is autumn, and winter bars the way to spring, I want to get my feet on the hard high road again, to once more engender a thirst which I must walk five weary miles to quench.

But there are ten months between me and these, and some have thirty days and some have thirty-one. Heigho!

The Convalescent

If I read the various noises aright, it must be nearly eleven o'clock. They shifted the only timepiece in the room when I had been here a few days, because I said the place was full of galloping horses. It was, too! They used to come out of a picture that hung just opposite the bed, and stampede round the room; then I used to pull the clothes over my head and scream.

So, as they have moved the clock, I have learnt to tell the time by the sounds which filter through from the outside world. First the sparrows on the roof; then the milkman; next the schoolbell—and that means nearly nine o'clock. At ten comes another milkman, whom I have christened the Melancholy Milkman, because he does nothing but drone in dolorous accents, "Fine noo milk!" It sounds like the cry "Bring out your dead!" Close on his heels (and this is half-past ten) comes the garrulous greengrocer, who recites a complete catalogue of his wares, from artichokes to onions, outside each house. If he should by chance omit any mention of kidneys (a variety of potato, I believe), he goes back and does it all over again. He is a conscientious man. When I am quite well I am going out to kill him.

By the time this fiend has wandered out of hearing, it is noon; and the children are out of school. I can hear them playing in the back gardens if it be fine. That shrill scream comes from my old friend Little-Winnie-over-the-Wall; and I expect she has tumbled from the swing. Everyday she sends kind inquiries with, "Please how is the ill gentleman, and has he got any cigarette pictures?"

Presently comes the clatter of plates from below; and I begin to speculate as to what they are having for lunch. But whatever it is, is not for me. "Slops" are to be my portion, seemingly, for eternity—

beef-tea and bread-and-milk; bread-and-milk and beef-tea, until they both taste alike. I have spoken to the doctor about it two or three times; but it makes no difference. I want something I can bite, something to crunch. "But we must be patient," he says. "We must persevere with the good, nourishing broths until we are a little stronger, and then, perhaps, a little chop." A little chop, indeed! Why, I am nearly as well as he is.

He stalks into the bedroom as if the place belonged to him; and puffs and blows, and says it is cold, or wet, or fine, as if that mattered to me; and puts his tall hat on the bed, from whence I have several times tried to dislodge it with my feet; and pokes me in the ribs and grins in what I suppose is his best bedside manner; and tells me I shall be about in a week. He has been telling me I shall be about in a week for months now. I suppose he is trying to cheer me up, poor chap.

But the endless hours I lie here make even his visits welcome. Through whole hours my mind seems numb, and I lie passive, while the day draws its slow length along. It all seems as if I were moving towards some climax; as if this weary waiting, waiting, were but the prelude to something greater, but a working out of some event, and that presently something would happen. But it never does; it never does!

Yesterday I counted all the art nouveau chrysanthemums on the wall-paper of one side of the room. There were three hundred and eleven—or was it three hundred and thirteen? Never mind! This afternoon, if the light lasts, I mean to do the whole room. That should fill up quite two hours. There is one flower where the paper has been joined up badly. It looks like an old man's head; and now I have seen the resemblance, it leers at me whenever I turn that way. The pattern on the window curtains, too, if looked at for long, takes on grotesque shapes, which, when they let me have a fire in the room, dance and gibber at me until I have to bury my face in the pillow. But that only happens towards evening, when the room is filled with that greyness that is neither light nor dark, and the dreary shadows pile up in the half-lit corners.

While daylight lasts I can see quite a lot of the outside world from my window. The view is made up of one chimney pot, about a square yard of sky, and the greater part of a black poplar. When I first began to notice things the poplar was well clad in leaves, just tinged with autumn. Now they have all dropped but two, which seem to have been forgotten. They hang, alone and cheerless, on the topmost twigs, flapping idly like the remnants of the decorations for some long passed pageant. Sometimes they tantalise me and I want to shake the tree, and let them flutter to their rest. Each morning I look for them, and I have prayed that in the night they should have fallen. If they would only drop, I think I could go to sleep …

Last week a friend came to see me, and brought something with him to read to me. I had been looking forward to this, but when I saw what the book was I am afraid I was rude to him. Boswell's Johnson, of all things! Boswell's Johnson for a sick man! Now, if it had been "Alice in Wonderland," or even "Treasure Island"—

When I was a small boy of ten a benevolent uncle took me to see the Mohawk Minstrels, and I have never forgotten that double semi-circle of immaculate shirt fronts, with the corner man bobbing up every few seconds to propound a conundrum. And when I read Boswell I invariably see him as that corner man starting from his seat to ask one of his never-failing stock of questions in order to give the doctor a chance of airing his heavy wisdom or making an epigram.

At the top of each page I seem to see:

"Boswell: Kin you tole me, Brudder Johnson, what am de—?"

A little more of this will make me frightened at my own shadow. There are a lot of noises in a bedroom; chairs creaking, cupboard doors trying to open, and a host of other little sounds whose cause I have tried in vain to find. Outside a dog will bark twice; then comes an interval, and another dog will answer. And now I lie in agony waiting for the first dog to bark again.

At night I find that the last thing I have any inclination for is sleep. I toss and turn on the furrowed bed, trying in vain to find a position which does not cause me to ache all over. I hear the man next door chain his dog up, while lower down the street a bolt is shot or a door barred; and slowly a deep silence creeps over all.

So I turn my hot pillow again, and prepare for the hideous night; a night of staring into the darkness, of trying to sleep until I curse aloud and watch my square yard of sky for the first grey signs of morning.

And when morning comes, it is the night I pray for.

The Art of Reading

On the back of my fire insurance policy there is set out a few of the many ways of setting fire to one's house—raking the hot embers on to the hearth, blowing down lamp chimneys, etc. The last item on the list is "reading and smoking in bed."

Now, if the insurance company will not let me read in bed, I refuse to renew my policy. Reading in bed is the second finest thing a man can do with his spare time in the winter. The first is sitting up in a hurry on a cold morning; and then, suddenly remembering that it is Sunday, getting under the clothes again. I have done that three times in an hour! Reading in bed is an art. You must first get a steady light, and that is not easy. Electric lamps are always fixed so that reading in bed is an impossibility. If this is not so, a man comes and alters them.

The same thing applies to gas; and candles bob and gutter and dwindle. For myself, I use a brass lamp with a broad, heavy base so that it cannot fall over. Once in bed, turn on your right side and double your pillow. Now pull the chair on which the lamp stands as near to the bed as possible. Then, with your left hand, pull the bed-clothes well up over your left ear, to shut out all external noises; hold your book in your right hand, and there you are. But you must not go to sleep, or the book may fall on the lamp, and then … That is what will happen to me some night, so my friends tell me. Some have given me instances, with illustrations from Foxe's "Book of Martyrs."

Another excellent way of reading, specially adapted to the perusal of large books with bountiful illustrations, is to lie at full length on the hearthrug before the fire; the book between your elbows, and your chin in your hands. Also, there should be chestnuts baking on the bottom bar, and a cat to sing by the fender. This is a favourite attitude with children, but why we should be expected to grow out of it I cannot say. Certainly, when one gets old it is not considered dignified; and there is sometimes a difficulty about getting up again. I made my first acquaintance with the "Arabian Nights" in this manner, and when the firelight danced and flickered the Djinns and Afrits would squeak and gibber on the pages.

In the summer you may assume the same position on the grass, preferably beside a stream. But here your surroundings are liable to distract your attention; and in the open air each book seems to require its own attitude. When on a holiday a good anthology of verse is a sweet companion.

There you will find pictures to fit whatever frame of mind you chance to be in; verses for the running brook, for the dark woods; for the uplands and the valleys; for the sea and the sky, the sun and the wind; songs to which the leaves will dance and caper, and madrigals with the magic of the thrush's pipe running through them. On a stile in Sussex I have renewed my acquaintance with Keats; on my back, beneath a high-rooted beech, I have retasted Wordsworth; and the rocks and breakers will make a glorious background for Longfellow.

Old Omar knew well what he was talking about; but it has always been a matter for regret with me that he did not find room for a pipe of tobacco in that happy twelfth quatrain.

I have tried reading whilst walking, but must write this down a failure. There are fences and ditches; and in town, lamp-posts. The only person who can read and walk at the same time is the errand boy. You will see him with a huge sack over his shoulder; ambling, not walking, along the pavement; sideways, like a crab for the most part; and devouring with every show of the deepest interest the contents of some grease-marked, grimy blood-curdler. At every hundred yards or so he will halt, still reading; and by this you may know that a climax— and there is usually one to every page—has been reached. Further progress is impossible until Dick Deadeye has drawn his bowie and dispatched another horde of yelling Sioux. The thrill over, he wanders on his way.

Newspapers can only be read in two places—at the breakfast-table and in the train. In the chilly air of the first few hours of the day, before the world is properly aired and fit to use, it is next to impossible to read anything but hard facts; or, at least, facts as hard as you can get them. That is why the breakfast hour has been fixed in all civilised homes immediately after the first post has come. Fancy trying to read poetry—Herrick, for instance—to the rattle of the coffee cups, and with the thunder of the toast you are eating crackling in your ears. The idea is absurd! But you can learn how Aunt Emma's Plymouth Rocks are laying, or all about the new Triple Alliance, with unruffled mind. Breakfast is a quarrelsome meal. We are not properly awake, and everything we see or hear is a challenge. Therefore, if you must read a book, choose one crammed with facts; a mathematical work, for instance. Nobody but a confirmed pessimist could possibly find fault with the statement that twice two are four.

It is all very well to say that we should wake up refreshed, invigorated, full of the joy of life, easy in body and mind. It cannot be done in London, at any rate. The people who feel like that in the early morning—in the winter, I mean—do not read books. They take guns out with them, and shoot things. And it is not the joy of life that makes them do so either; it is brutality and lust after blood.

For fireside reading, if you are not allowed to lie on the rug, an armchair is, of course, the only other position of comfort. And comfortable armchairs are more than rubies and scarcer than the dodo. Mine is a beauty, with a big, fat back, and a wonderful seating capacity—a very Falstaff of armchairs, sleek and smiling, inviting one to its warm embrace. The firelight winks and blinks in its polished legs, and its corpulent shadow fills half the room. No matter what my mood, how disagreeable or worried I am, I have only to slip on my old, frayed Norfolk jacket, with matches in every pocket and pipes in most, and drop into that chair, and I become another person. I take on a new set of emotions. The petty worries seem to slip away from me; and when my briar is well alight I wander from things mundane, and move in a new world—a world peopled with the puppets of my book.

And if it should be my old, dirty, paperbacked "Treasure Island" I have chanced on, I find that I can still squirm in my seat when John Silver stumps on deck; which at least proves that I am not getting old.

These few methods of reading which I have instanced are useful only when one is in search of amusement; reading to meet old friends or to make new ones. Reading for knowledge, for profit, is no more like reading for pleasure than seeing chickens crammed by machinery is like watching a goldfinch swaying on the top of a thistle, the while he pecks the seeds therefrom.

So you may read your "Origin of Species" any silly way you like.

Shop Windows

As a small boy, when watching the raindrops chasing one another down the window got monotonous, and "Jessica's First Prayer" failed to brighten the dreary prospect of a wet Sunday afternoon, one of my favourite occupations was spending a five-pound note—on paper. What sharp knives I bought, and what gorgeous apples; what beautiful smoothing planes, and magic lanterns; what real watches and real steam-engines, worked by real steam! By the time the list totalled up to £4 18s., my conscience began to worry me; and I hurriedly spent the remaining florin on a new dress or a gold-mounted umbrella for some aunt or uncle. This in order to prove to myself my own unselfishness.

It is partly this love of pretending that makes us stop and stare in shop windows, well knowing that we do not intend to purchase anything. It is really surprising what a lot of things there are in the world that one can do without; and to fully appreciate this you should go on a Barmecide shopping expedition.

Everybody likes looking in shop windows, except those people who have money to spend. They go straight inside the shop, ask for what they want, get it, and come out again. But this is not looking at the shops; it is merely buying things, and he who does it is missing a lot.

Some years ago I could not pass a tobacconist's window without stopping to admire the big cubes of brown leaf, all tied with green and orange ribbons; the stacks and pyramids of cigarettes wrought into marvellous windmills and castles. But one day I saw such a window being dressed, and discovered, to my sorrow, that those same generous bales of "Peep o' Day" Returns were each but a thin layer of tobacco glued over a box; that those huge piles of cigarettes were hollow cylinders of paper, dummies; and now these things have lost their savour.

After this discovery I began to be suspicious of other displays, and not without cause. But, although the grocer puts packets of sawdust in his window, most of his goods are above suspicion. There is poetry in his Himalayas of White Crystals, his cascades of dried prunes, and piles of candied peel decked with long strips of cinnamon from Ceylon. The window of such a shop at Christmas-time always recalls to me the "Eve of St. Agnes," with its

> Manna and dates, in argosy transferr'd
> From Fez; and spiced dainties, every one,
> From silken Samarcand to cedar'd Lebanon.

Chemists, if they stick to the row of white jars with mysterious names on them, and the three large bottles of blue and green and red, can still rely on my patronage. From the edge of the pavement one can get admirable pantomime effects, as the passers-by stream through the three broad beams of coloured light. In chemists' windows, too, you will sometimes see those automatic advertising devices, which are at once the joy of the small boy and the despair of the policeman. One I know, where a corpulent monk consumes gallons of cod liver oil every few seconds, and when he has removed the bottle from his lips, three stiff jerks bring his right hand into play, and he strokes his gaberdine and rolls his eyes with lifelike satisfaction. I like watching that monk, but I mistrust his bottle. I was never so demonstrative over cod liver oil myself.

Most people have a shop that they like to look in. Some prefer watching wax dolls working sewing machines, or sewing machines working waxen dolls, whichever it is. Others are attracted by boots temptingly displayed with trimmings of stuffed grouse and real heather, or boots sawn through the middle to show that their soles are all leather. This is probably true of the boot that is sawn through. Others, again, and these hunt in couples, will make a bee line for a furniture shop, for no other purpose than to see if the suite they like so much is still there, and to look at one another, and smile, and blush. It takes no very discerning eye to find out what is the matter with them.

Flower shops I can always find time for; but in winter they make me sad. It is not right that roses should be dragged out of their proper season and made to bloom in our ghastly December. Born before their due time, they look fragile, tender, consumptive almost; and if I worked in one of those shops I should be afraid to open the door for fear they caught cold and died. But every winter sees them, each pure bloom gemmed with pearls of moisture, which I believe the young lady behind the counter puts on with a fountain-pen filler before she opens the shop. And in summer—? No, even in summer, I do not like flower shops. Flowers have no business in shops. I have seen carnations and lilies, roses and forget-me-nots, violets and cowslips (Sumer is i-comen in, Loude sing cuccu!), drooping their heads with fatigue; and sighing, yea, I have heard them sighing and seen them weeping, for the warm breeze across the heath, the whisper of the brook, and the cool of the evening dew. And I have sighed and wept with them!

Book shops I dare not look into. The names on the volumes, the fat backs of them, the pages cunningly opened at some interesting passage or picture, the fine editions of my old mean paperbacks— these I may not stop to look at, or I must fall. There is always in the window the very book I want; for your bookseller has a wonderful knowledge of human nature, and casts his flies with marvellous skill. I have never got out of a book shop under five shillings; and when buying books, it is the books that one really cannot afford that one buys.

Of all the uses to which a window can be put, the greatest is undoubtedly the frying of sausages. Five minutes spent watching those browning cylinders bursting with plenty, the curling steam and the odorous onions squirming and twisting in the enamel dishes, and the "mashed," the beautiful flowery "mashed," all decked with parsley— this makes me as hungry as a hunter. But I always go somewhere else to lunch.

A woman seldom looks in a shop window, except in the way of strict business. Certainly she goes shop-gazing, but drapers, milliners, and dressmakers monopolise her attention, and if she buys nothing, she plans. Now that toque, she thinks, with a touch of red just there; or that straw, if the feather were only put so— Then, with a glance in the mirror which forms the background to the display, and another quick look at the hat in question, she has mentally seen herself in it, has fixed it in her mind, and straightway scurries home to rebend, reconstruct, and redecorate last year's discarded shell.

I once saw a woman looking in a tailor's shop, and marvelled thereat. True, thought I, she might be going to buy a fancy vest for— But even as I thought, she gave her head a quick jerk, and, using the window for a mirror, tugged at her blouse until it covered the band of her skirt, patted her back hair twice, tilted her hat a trifle, and was gone.

"Mother Shippey's"

There was ever but one way of going down Bridge-st., and it was accomplished in this wise. First you stopped at the little front window on the right to watch old Toomey mending boots; and when he had filled his mouth with brass brads it was part of the ritual to flatten your nose against the glass, and watch him splutter. I often wonder why he never died of this. The next stop was across the road at the wood yard, where the screaming logs are eaten up by the greedy circular saw. Here you always contrived to snatch a handful of the pungent sawdust, destined to go down the collar of the next boy you met.

At the top of the hill came the last and best halt of all. No self-respecting boy passed Mother Shippey's without giving her window at least five minutes, even though his pockets wore as empty as a pair of bellows, and his next week's allowance mortgaged to the last farthing. For here were displayed those beautiful greeny glass jars filled with sweets ("suckers" we called them), of all colours, shapes, and prices; red and white striped sticks, saffron creams with pink tops, and flat tin dishes of lucent candy. Here, too, was toffee in all its many variations—toffee plain, toffee with a fair sprinkling of nuts on its surface, toffee with shreds of cokernut gleaming in its amber heart, and toffee piled with real almonds, mountains high. Shades of my lost teeth, but Mother Shippey knew how to make toffee nearly as well as she knew how to seduce the sparse pennies from our pockets!

None of her dainties were ticketed, and she had no names for them. We christened them all, and did it as only boys could. There was "cow-heel" and "parrot's food," "cast-iron" and "jelly babies," "fog-drops" and "doormat," "nightmares" and "sudden death." But "doormat" was the only one which in any way earned the name we had bestowed upon it. You have seen those gelatine lozenges, semi-transparent discs of a glue-like compound, which are sometimes used to repair cracks in windows. These, it appears, are punched from a large sheet of this same material, leaving behind a perforated slab. This is "doormat"; and it was three ounces for a penny and very indigestible. It was plastic, in consistency not unlike India-rubber, and it lent itself admirably to the purposes of art. Beautiful caricatures of the head could be carved out of it with a penknife, under cover of a Latin prose exercise; and it could be pulled and pushed into all manner of astounding shapes. Quite the last thing we did with "doormat" was to eat it!

Then there were marsh-mallows which melted almost before you had got them to your mouth, and peppermint balls, after eating which you drew in your breath, and so obtained that delicious cool effect at the back of your tongue.

But who shall write the praises of Mother Shippey's stone ginger; that muddy liquid which gurgled so musically into the thick glasses on those hot evenings when you had been fielding all the afternoon in the sun; that wonderful nectar which, despite the weather, was always cool? And, oh, the happy moments of anticipation, while you waited for the froth to go down!

The old dame herself did not enter into our lives more than was necessary for the transaction of business. Amongst the younger boys rumour had it that she was a kind of amateur witch. This probably gained credence from the fact that when Franklin Tertius gorged himself with fruit, and sat disconsolate and in pain on a sugar-box in the shop, Mother Shippey administered a stinking decoction to him, which removed the pain in half an hour. From this it speedily went round that the old woman juggled with herbs and simples. Also, she had a marvellous memory, and would grin and cackle and show her one tooth when she reminded you of the fourpence you owed her from last term.

For her face, it was that of a gargoyle; all wrinkled and seamed with age; and her chin grew a beard like to a stubble field at harvest time. But we forgave her all this, for that she dispensed most excellent wares, and did not unduly press for payment.

When last I went down Bridge-st. the old Adam pulled me up outside Toomey's window, and Toomey's son filled his mouth with brass brads just as did his father before him. But I found that I had forgotten how to make the necessary face at him; or perhaps I had grown too respectable. Crossing the road, I heard the circular saw whirr and groan; and its groan grew to a wail, and its wail to a crescendo shriek, just as it always did; and its shriek died down to a groan and a whirr, just as it always did.

But at the top of the hill came disillusionment. Mother Shippey, whom we knew could never die, just as surely as we knew she had never been born, was gone. Some bloated capitalist had bought her out, and seeking to trade on her reputation, had fixed over the shop window that all might see the legend, "Mother Shippey." Now, this name, which had been handed down to us by our predecessors, and was one of the traditions of the school, was a thing sacred and apart, and not for the public eye or ear. We did not even know that the old woman's name was Shippey. Some forgotten genius had probably so christened her, and the title had stuck through we knew not how many generations. And if you could have seen her you would have agreed that it was the only name possible for her. Of course her name was Mother Shippey! How could it have been anything else?

Yet here it was, blazoned abroad in letters of brass; shouted from the shop-front for the town louts to laugh at.

And the window? Well, there was no "doormat," because that was the first thing I looked for; neither was there any "cow-heel" or "parrot's food"; nor anything that a boy would be likely to dignify with a nickname. Creams there were of sickly colours; toffee cut into geometrically-correct cubes; abominations with names like noyeau, nougat, and marzipan; but no toffee in slabs, no hard-bake, no sugar-candy with a string running through the middle.

Some of these new-fangled arrangements were put up in boxes and tied with pink and blue ribbons. How Mother Shippey would have clucked if anyone had suggested ribbons to her!

And the glaring colours of the sweets! Not ripe browns and warm reds and pure whites; but hideous greens and scarlets, and pale aesthetic, washed-out tints the obvious product of the chemical works.

I looked into the shop, but I knew already what I should see. Behind the counter stood a cigarette-picture girl, her hair done into the latest shape, and she hummed a music-hall ditty. Round her left wrist there hung two bracelets, each carrying about ten shillings' worth of threepenny pieces, which jingled like the trappings of a circus horse when she moved, and the front of her blouse was hidden behind a multitude of brooches.

I hope, for the honour of the old school, that none of the present boys deal there. But they would be afraid of Mother Shippey haunting them!

The Art of the Pipe

One of those energetic people who are perpetually "tidying up" and making things in a muddle by so doing has been at work in my room. Inquiry after three pipes, which were the first things I missed, elicited the information that they had been given to the dustman. To the dustman! My beloved briars, two bent and one straight! Oh, most lame and impotent conclusion—to be choked with rank shag and sucked by a dustman!

Pipes—that is, old pipes—should never be given away. They should be collected, like old love-letters. Unlike love-letters, however, they should not be tied into bundles and stowed away in the bottom drawer, but left lying scattered, two on the mantelpiece, one on the windowsill, another on the table, the rest being distributed about the room as fancy guides. Neither should one use a pipe-rack. For the same reason, walking-sticks should never be put into umbrella-stands. Umbrellas certainly, for it is impossible to be sentimental about an umbrella. Sticks should stand in the corners of rooms where you may sit and gaze on them, and dream of dusty roads and steep climbs, of shouting winds and pleasant shades.

Pipes, I say, should be left lying about where you can pick them up and fondle them. Their associations will justify the litter they make. This charred and battered relic it was that took you all through Wiltshire last summer; that one, with the graceful bowl and deeply-bitten mouthpiece, helped you through those terrible hours when you paced back and forth beneath the windows, awaiting the doctor's verdict of life or death …

Somehow, each of my pipes seems to have one outstanding association; to recall one definite incident from a host of minor recollections. Here is one which I never handle but I think of a certain broken gate about a mile out of Rye, just before you begin the long tramp across the Marsh. Another always conjures up one of Lamb's essays, "Mrs. Battle's Opinions on Whist," but the reason for this I cannot trace. Yet a third is connected in my mind with an inn at Wittersham and bread and cheese and cool beer, a sun-bonnet, and a pretty face.

The man who smokes for pure pleasure seldom chooses any other medium than the pipe; and of pipes, the briar is the most comforting.

You take the favourite of the moment from your pocket, give its glossy bowl a caress on your coat-sleeve, put it between your teeth, and take a few preliminary puffs to see that everything is in working order. Then, filling it, you put your feet on the fender, slip as low as possible in your chair, and watch the curling vapours weaving ladders to the skies. It is by these ladders that smokers climb to heaven.

This is the only way to use tobacco. There are others, but they are mere flirtations compared with the serious lovemaking of a bent briar. Cigars require removing from the lips far too frequently, and cigarettes are too transient—no sooner alight than they drop their ash down one's waistcoat, and in another moment or so are too short to smoke with comfort.

Unless a man keep a valet or have unlimited wealth, a meerschaum is out of the question. I was once presented with one of these luxuries, and the fortnight that I smoked it was, I think, the most trying I have ever lived through. I would step from the pavement to the road to let people pass; would hold that cursed pipe in my mouth with shaking hand and tremble when in a crowd. Before sitting down, I would carefully search all my pockets to find its whereabouts, and I lived in deadly fear of hearing that crunch which would tell me the bowl had caved in. But one night I sat at home reading and smoking, until, carried away by my book, I unconsciously leaned forward, and, as is my custom with a briar, smote the meerschaum three resounding raps on the top bar of the fireplace.

I was not sorry, for the nervous strain had been frightful. Amber also comes under this ban; it is too precious, too tender for such an every-day purpose as smoking, and, so far as I can see, is only useful to keep flies in. Smoking a meerschaum-and-amber pipe must be rather like playing nap with a Fellow of the Royal Society—the gorgeousness of it takes away all the pleasure. With a meerschaum, too, smoking for smoking's sake is in danger of becoming a side issue, the chief object of such a pipe being to acquire colour. There is the stealthy glance at the bowl to see how it is progressing, and the temptation to smoke, wanting the desire. This also applies to those new-fangled monstrosities known as calabashes. Fancy calling a pipe a calabash! It sounds like the name of a new South American Republic. And then the frantic shape of the things—up and over, and round and round, like a French horn, and bound at the mouth with metal, as the sawn-off tusk of a circus elephant is bound. Their proper place is a grocer's window, with oranges and pineapples and melons tumbling from their gaping maws. I have no longing whatever to smoke a cornucopia.

A pipe in a man's mouth always makes him look good-tempered and at peace. If Hamlet had smoked a bent briar, I am sure he would not have been so melancholy. He would have taken things more easily, and not have worried and fretted as he did.

Or, again, take Falstaff. What better would suit that cheery old rogue, that full-bellied toper, than a long churchwarden, curving downwards to his ample belt? And swaggering Pistol should smoke a short black clay, which, when not in use, he would tuck reverently in the band of his bonnet.

When women smoke they are always theatrical, flourishing their dainty cigarette like a rapier, blowing the smoke with puffed-out cheeks, and giggling and coughing, and protesting that they like it immensely, but always throwing away the larger portion, and never attempting a pipe.

With your true smoker, his briar is part of his face, as human, as intelligent as any other of his features. I have known men the contour of whose faces demanded a pipe, whose profile did not seem complete without one.

But, I can hear you saying, this man carries the thing to extremes; he makes a fad of it. That is as you please; only I love my pipes just as you love your dogs. Yes, and I have even given them names, too!

And now I am going to the town hall to find out where our dustman lives.

The Art of Dress

With the first upward thrust of the daffodil's green spears, man, like some of the lower animals, begins to think of changing his drab winter coat for something more in keeping with the triumphal march of the lengthening days. To that end he frequents tailors' shops; and carries home books of patterns to be felt and pinched and twisted and stretched, first by himself and then by his wife. They wag their wise heads, and talk of tweeds and serges, as though they had been brought up at the looms and knew their subject, warp and woof.

Next he is measured, and never did he feel so puny. He sees a smile on the tailor's lips as the tape is run round his chest, but draw he never so long a breath he cannot quite reach the 36. Two or three days later he calls to be fitted, and is clothed in a garment made of sackcloth and pins, horrible to look at, and still more horrible to get into. In a week the completed suit is sent home, hung across a chair to remove the creases, and on the following Sunday is worn for the first time.

And now begins a week or so of poignant agony; of imagining that people are looking at him, that he is conspicuous; that his coat is much too long, or his trousers much too short. He spends several minutes each day craning his neck to get a glimpse of his south aspect, and until the newness of the thing has worn off is as one wearing the Shirt of Nessus.

If you watch the men who go to church on Sunday mornings you will notice a certain stiffness about their bearing. There is a suggestion of growing pains in the action of their knees; and you can fancy they creak as they bend their bodies to sit down. This is due to the fact that all new suits for the first few weeks of their career are known as "best clothes," and worn only when attending church or visiting friends.

When the clothes have been worn a month or so the crease down the front of the trousers becomes less marked, and from this date their decline begins. For perhaps another two or three weeks the careful man tries to accentuate this crease by placing his trousers between the mattresses of his bed—by far the cheapest and finest trousers press ever invented. But even this soon fails, and the suit is relegated to the shabby-genteel limbo of "second best."

Too soon it descends from this stage to become common "everydays," and by then it is beginning to grow old. It is also just beginning to become comfortable.

There is not that familiarity, that friendliness about new clothes that there is about old. It is as if your coat did not know you, had not been introduced. It stands aloof; prim, well-ordered, stiff, and unsociable. The best way is to take no notice of this, to snub your garments as they seem to snub you; and in a month or so you will find they have lost their straight lines and taken on graceful curves; that they now fit you, move with you, and are part of you. In two or three weeks your trousers will bag at the knees, and you will no longer be afraid to stoop for fear of making them baggy. Your waistcoat will have acquired the correct number of wrinkles down its front; and the pockets of your coat will hold all you want to put in them, which is ten times more than they were ever expected to hold.

The science of dress is the wearing of new clothes, the study of times and seasons, of curves, and fit and fashion. The art of dress is the wearing of old clothes, the study of ease and comfort, entailing the loss of your neighbours' respect and the disgust of your wife. The art of dress is therefore seldom practised outside one's home.

When a button comes off science says you must leave that suit at home and wear another; art says dig a hole in the cloth, push the brace through, and use a nail.

The man who employs a valet, whose cocoon is spun round him by a hired servant, cannot afford to wear old clothes, and in this he misses many of the minor pleasures of life. He never learns how to trim the fringe from the bottom of his trouser legs; how to rejuvenate a tired bowler hat with ink; how so to manipulate a shabby tie that its brightest spot comes to the fore; or how a well-brushed overcoat covers a multitude of shiny patches. But what is worst of all, he never has the pleasure of cleaning his own boots. Boot-cleaning is the finest possible cure for the early morning hump. When your liver is out of order, and you get up half asleep with murder in your eye; when the letter you expected is not under your breakfast-plate, and your shaving water is cold; when the whole of mankind seem pitted against you, and life takes on a sombre hue; then clean all the boots in the house.

There are not many men who can be miserable while cleaning boots. Some whistle, others hum or sing, and nearly all walk about. Consequently one of the chief essentials to the proper enjoyment of this pastime is a garden. Then, with a boot on your left hand and a brush in your right, you saunter down one path and up another, planting roses here and dahlias there, irises in the shadow of the wall, and a crimson rambler over the summer-house. Still polishing, you stoop over the small glass frame to inspect the little cemetery of seeds, buried in regiments; each with its epitaph inscribed on a little wooden memorial at the head of the rank. A gap in the palings requiring a little amateur carpentry is next noticed. And so you wander round, making mental notes, and arranging for future long evenings and early risings, until both your boots are done, and you are once again in your right mind. That is, of course, providing you have not missed your train.

Quite the opposite effect is produced by the brushing of clothes. Boots, you must understand, can only be in one of two conditions. Either they are good and fit to wear, or they are bad. In the latter case they are not worn, and therefore are not cleaned.

But clothes have many stages on their road to decay, in each of which they are wearable. They can be new, when brushing them is a pleasure; or fairly new, when they leave you indifferent. They can be shabby, when they make you mourn; or old, when the minute examination which brushing entails causes you to swear. You see the frayed edges, the shiny places, the straggling threads where a button has been lost; and every time you brush them you see them hastening to their end.

And although it is customary to have boots soled and heeled, yet it is not considered correct to wear patched clothes.

For the purposes of business a man does not wear what he likes, but what his employer thinks fit. I know an office where a fancy waistcoat would mean the sack; arguing an intimacy with bookmakers and barmaids, and consequent raids on the petty cash. During business hours we must dress conventionally. But at home, in the evening, when the fire is made up, the slippers beside the fender, and the dog asleep on the rug; then the wise man puts on old clothes, companionable clothes. At the very least he dons an old jacket, in the pocket of which he knows he will find the paperback he was reading last night, and the disreputable old pipe his wife will not allow him to smoke out of doors.

By now, a tailor would consider his appearance disgraceful, and it probably is. But he is supremely comfortable. For clothes, and carpet slippers, and pipes, are not worth anything until they are worth nothing.

The Post

Coming down to breakfast one day last week I found awaiting me a letter from a friend, describing at length a walk he had taken over the Downs on one of those mornings when spring runs shouting across the hills.

Now I had lain abed just a little too long that day; had gashed my chin when shaving; and was walking about with my head held high lest there should be blood upon my collar. Outdoors, a grey rain and a cold wind. So I was not in the best of humours. And when I read how my friend had found the lesser celandine in a sheltered combe; how in the heart of a coppice that I know well, he had knelt before a clump of primroses; then I stamped my feet and could have broken things.

This man, I told myself, was an egregious ass; his letter drivel; and I hurled from the house to be rude to office boys.

But that evening, in my armchair by the fire, I read his letter again; and went every step of the way, too! And reading, I wondered if the ash were in flower yet, or the blue tits nesting. When really interesting letters containing news or gossip arrive by the first post, they should be put aside for perusal in the evening. At the breakfast-table one is not in a fit state of mind to give them that attention which is their due.

Aunt Charlotte, we will say, writes from home to tell you that old Mr. Grimes is dead; that one of the Prentice girls, she is not sure which, is going to marry the vicar; that the lantern lecture last week was a "huge success." She then finishes her letter by writing across the first page, until the result looks like wire-netting run mad. All aunts do this! Tucking the letter back into its envelope you notice the postscript. It is written on the inside of the flap of the envelope, and as you have burst this with your thumb in opening it is probably unreadable. However, with the aid of a knife you manage to get the flap undone and pieced together; to read, "Do you know of any good books?" Here the proper thing to do is to scream, or cram your serviette into your mouth. It may save you going mad!

But consider the reception of this same letter if you had put it in your pocket when it arrived, and read it at night, after dinner. You are sorry about old Mr. Grimes. You remember one day when he caught you in his raspberry canes. And the Prentice girls? Let's see, that must be Maud your aunt writes of. Pretty girl, Maud! Down drops the letter to your knee, and you stare into the fire; sigh or smile, according to the circumstances, and read on.

If there is one kind of letter more than another which should not be read in the morning it is the love-letter. No man can feel romantic at the breakfast-table. Greedy, cynical, or bloodthirsty if you like; but never romantic, seldom even affectionate. Therefore the careful man will sort his correspondence, opening his business letters only; a fitting accompaniment to the harsh crackle of toast, or the banality of eggs and bacon. It is almost as bad to read a love-letter in the cold, grey hours of early morning as it is to write one at that unseemly time of day. As a matter of fact, I believe that so far at the male correspondent is concerned the majority of his amatory epistles are written during business hours; but never in the morning, always after lunch. I used to write mine in the friendly shelter of the "bought" ledger, and became quite expert at totting up long columns of figures at a moment's notice when I heard the head clerk creeping round the office. But most of the finest love-letters have been written in the evening, by the fire or in the garden, and as far as possible they should be read under the same conditions.

When Keats was writing those pitiful letters to Fanny Brawne he was often in deadly fear of being found out; of somebody peering over his shoulder and discovering his heart-beats. To avoid this possibility he would leave the superscription until the letter was written, filling it in the last thing before closing his note. This little ruse he naively pointed out to his correspondent, one of his letters commencing:

My dearest girl (I do not write this till the last, that no eye may catch it).

Letter-writing as an art must die out; and I doubt if the next generation will have the pleasure of peeping into the private lives of many of our great men, through the medium of those fat, well-annotated volumes which Lamb, Dickens, and Carlyle have bequeathed to us. Few people sit down nowadays to turn out page after page of delightful gossip; and even if this were not so, still fewer would feel disposed to read it. When one can travel almost from one side of London to the other for the price of a penny stamp, allowing a small margin for exaggeration, what need of a voluminous correspondence?

The whole scheme of letter-writing, as described by Stevenson in a note to Sidney Colvin, is that you "sit down every day and pour out an equable stream of twaddle." And that is all done with! When there is news our friends in London jump on a bus; those in the country send us a local paper. For speed is the god we bow before, and neither good letter-writing nor reading will admit of speed. Perhaps there are two exceptions to this last rule; the perusal of income-tax papers, and notes from neighbours whom your dog has bitten. These should, of course, be read at breakfast-time, when you will stick the first behind the pipe-rack, and return the second endorsed, "I do not keep a dog!"

The Choice of a Profession

Even as the grass in the next field is always the greenest, the view from the next hilltop always the best, so the profession which the other man follows seems always to be the very one we are most fitted for. And the reason for this is not far to seek. Few of us are in the habit of talking much of our failures. Our successes, the advantages of the trade we follow, its short hours, its good pay, its freedom from worry; these we brag about to our intimate friends, just as we brag about our excellent train service, the length of our garden, or the sagacity of our dog.

Consequently our friends see only the bright side of our business affairs and covet them for their own. There is a glamour about the other man's job which we can seldom find in ours. The boy whose sole aim in life is to be an engine-driver is attracted, not by the wages, the hard work, the long hours, but by the idea of commanding an engine, of having that great iron beast under his control, and by the irresistible fascination of speed and action. It is doubtful if the engine-driver is aware of these attractions, but for the boy they constitute the job. He wants to be master of something, to guide and rule. Thus, when we played "trains" on the landing with three chairs and the photograph album for the driver's seat, the fun of the thing lay in the controlling of our train, the flag-waving and whistle-blowing; the stopping and starting by the pulling of levers made with walking-sticks.

As a boy, the dangling rope at the back of the carrier's van was the candle round which I hovered. I longed to cultivate that monkey-like agility with which the vanboy swung from instant death to the tailboard of the van, whistling the while. But I lost this unholy desire after seeing such a boy carry what looked like a grand piano up a flight of stairs. After all, a glow-worm, when we hold it in our hands, is only a nasty little beetle!

Few of us are contented with our trades. We could always do better at something else. Ask any man what he would most like to be, and the answer is invariably other than he is. He who says he is contented with his lot thinks contentment a virtue, and assumes it, though he has it not. The really contented man has nothing to strive for, and as strife is the salt of life, he must lead a frightfully humdrum existence. A turnip is about the only thing I can think of which is likely to be absolutely contented, to have no ambition. And yet, on second thoughts, I suppose, if it had its way, a turnip would sooner run to seed and propagate its kind than garnish boiled mutton.

For myself, I have two pet professions which I should like to follow; and they attract me, not so much by the money I might make as by the mental and bodily comfort and ease they would provide. And I know I should make a ghastly failure of either. In the winter I desire nothing more than to keep a second-hand bookshop, and when the summer comes I would be a gamekeeper. For me the first means merely handling old and choice books, dipping into the still fresh wells of knowledge dug by ancient sages, and reading, perpetually reading. I should hate to sell a book I had not read!

For the second, the sole business of a gamekeeper, so far as I am concerned, is to walk through dark woods and by quiet waters, seeking for first flowerings and early birds' eggs; fostering young broods and making friends with all the rabbits on the estate, to the detriment of the kitchen garden. Of course, I know that gamekeeping means other and more arduous employment than this, but that is all I intend it shall mean for me. The muddiest of pools will look blue at a distance.

Fortunately, perhaps, few of us have any actual choice in the matter of our professions. When we were children absurd people used to call on Sunday afternoons to drink tea. Friends of the family they were, but to us never anything but awful men and women smothered in best clothes and with scent on their handkerchiefs. The men were very careful of their coat-tails when they sat down, and the women kept their hats on, sitting on the edge of a chair while their eyes roved round the room, putting prices on the furniture. And these visitors, who surely had sawdust in their veins in place of blood, would say every five minutes, "Well, my little man, and what are you going to be when you grow up?" To which the answer was anything from the captain of a Greenland whaler to a street orderly-boy.

It is seldom that these youthful aspirations are realised. Boys who run away to sea do not get more than two miles from home before they are smitten by hunger or remorse, and return to become clerks and grocer's assistants. But they still keep to their dreams, and the dreams of grown men are beautiful dreams. They have more common-sense and are more practical than the dreams of youth.

It all amounts to this. We do not choose our professions. For the majority of us they are chosen by our parents or dictated by circumstances; and instead of being able to adapt our circumstances to our desires, we are forced to modify our desires to fit in with our circumstances.

This is as it should be, for if we were granted our most heartfelt wishes, we might become contented; and for the contented man there are no dreams, no green oases in the arid desert of his life whereat his starved soul may feed and drink. In fact, a contented mind being a continual feast, the owner of it is in danger of putting on flesh, becoming a sidesman or a town councillor, and dying one bright morning as he runs to catch a train.

So let us all try to do our duty in that state of life unto which it has pleased fate to call us; and to each his dreams, his bookshop, his farm, or his neighbour's job.

The South Country

I suppose it would have been Sussex in any case. The first bright day in March brought the matter up, as a fine day out of season always does. You are sitting in the train, bound for the office; compassed about with cold feet and chilblains. Looking out of the window you chance to see an evergreen shrub marvellously lit with pale fire. It is the blessed sun, the first time you have seen it for ages; and you go to work inwardly disturbed. To-morrow all is grey and wet once more, and the feeling dies out. In a day or two spring gets its breath again, and comes on apace. Three more fair days will find you discussing, planning, and working hard to fill up the only two weeks in the year when you belong to you. During the other fifty you are hired out; your soul is in pawn. Soon you spend spare half-hours overhauling your cycle or inspecting your walking boots and giving them grease. Easter brings a trial trip, and you return to harness, grumbling and frothing at the bit.

On this morning in March a clump of hazel wands, old friends of mine, decked themselves with woolly "lambs' tails," and seeing them I sniffed luxuriously. And there came upon me that longing for big things; for wide stretches of sky and broad sweeps of meadowland; for the unconfined hills and the limitless sea. Now I know why Falstaff, dying in Eastcheap, babbled of green fields. Somebody must have walked past his window with a bunch of wild thyme.

That night two of us gathered round a map and made up our minds a score of times; suggesting, arguing, fighting almost; and choosing stray countries to take our rest in. We would cross the Channel to Dieppe and so wander through Normandy, or we would go to the Broads and wear a silk kerchief instead of braces. Anon we spoke of the New Forest, Wales, and Cornwall; of Derbyshire, Brittany, and the Belgian Ardennes.

Then came Mr. Brabant's book, and it was Sussex! But I suppose it would have been Sussex in any case, for, no matter how we may be impregnated with London, steeped in its grime, and suffocated between its piles of bricks, the instinct of the homing pigeon is in us all, and a Sussex man left on London-bridge to wander at his own sweet will could not go North. The Weald and the Downs would draw him along the Walworth-rd. Talk to him of Ditchling Beacon, Chanctonbury Ring, Pevensey Levels, and Romney Marsh, and you shall see his soul peer from his eyes. For such a man there is but one holiday, and it lies between Chichester and the Kent Ditch.

> Though all the rest were all my share,
>   With equal soul I'd see
> Her nine-and-thirty sisters fair,
>   Yet none more fair than she.
> Choose ye your need from Thames to Tweed,
>   And I will choose instead
> Such lands as lie 'twixt Rake and Rye,
>   Black Down and Beachy Head.

So, with this book and the Ordnance map we plodded here and there; and smiled at half-forgotten names; and told stories beginning "Remember when—?" We reminded each other of little hamlets lost in the hollows of the Downs, forgotten by Time; of the Long Man of Wilmington and the tinkle of sheep-bells. With chapter headings for sign-posts we found our way to Pevensey and the Conqueror, to Arundel and siege and slaughter, to Heathfield and Jack Cade, to Cuckmere and smuggling. We read and lived with the Flint men and their gods, with Caesar and his legions from Gaul, and sat in the shade of mills that ground corn when Domesday Book was clean.

The people of St. Leonard's Forest, where the serpentines and demi-cannon once came from, have a proverb which says that Sussex folk in exile sleep easier when their feet are turned towards their homes. But your pure Down and Weald and Marsh men seldom go far "into England," as leaving the county is called.

There is much in this book that I would Mr. Brabant had kept to himself. For he has told you of holy little places which you will presently find for yourselves, and then I must needs go and play elsewhere. Soon I shall be choked by the dust of your cycles as you buzz, all unseeing, through Graffham; or pale before the stench of motors come to defile the little breezes in the fir clumps of Gill's Lap. That is the one fault of the book. It has done things too well and left little or nothing unexplored. Next summer you will bring your tracing paper and your heel-ball, and take away our brasses; or, guided by the author, steal from the haunts of men to wonder at our oak rood-screens, our Transition-Norman arches and Early Geometrical windows.

Already you have laid your heavy hand on our coast-line, scarring it in many places. You took that little fishing village, "Brighthelmstone, near Lewes," and choked it with houses and people and picture postcards and called it Brighton. Not content with that, you nicknamed it "London-by-the-Sea." Barbarians! Again, in fifty years you have moved Eastbourne a mile nearer the cliff-edge and made it such that tall silk hats are worn there on Sundays. But, heaven be praised, you have so far overlooked Udimore and Billinghurst, Heyshott and Winchelsea. You have forgotten also a little bay where the ribs of a sunken ship stick through the sand at low water; where, on the cliffs above, I have seen a shepherd making traps for wheatears in the close-bit turf; where a south-westerly gale will change the shape of the coast-line with every tide, and where salmon-bass dance on top of the water and rabbits look at you and are not afraid. But where it is I shall not tell you, because presently I am going there and I do not want you.

"Rambles in Sussex." By F. G. Brabant. London, 1909: Methuen. 6s. net.

On Being Barbered

On those red-letter days when I have plenty of time in which to catch my train, it is my custom, if an event happening with such rarity can ever become a custom, to stop and look in the window of a certain cutler's shop. But it is not to admire the wooden round of horribly underdone beef, with carving-knife and fork laid atop; nor to see the gleaming razors and chisels and penknives cunningly arranged in circles like the old swords at the Tower. Besides these attractions there is in the window a magic mirror, a circular glass which, when looked into, distorts the gazer's visage into something almost offensive. And it is to stare, Narcissus-like, into this mirror that I sometimes stop on my way.

Reflected in its concave surface my face no longer resembles anything human; my head blots out the sky and darkness covers the earth. Gargantua was a pigmy, a goblin compared to me; and I feel as the people of Lilliput must have felt when Gulliver strode amongst them. Do I open my mouth, the top of my head is in danger of falling off, so great is the resulting upheaval. And the acres and acres of face stretching away and yet away into the beyond! I have no desire, as Alice had, to climb through and explore this looking-glass world. I should be eaten up or trampled underfoot.

No matter how closely I shave, my chin inspected in this magic glass carries as many spikes as the barrel of a musical-box. One morning I shaved twice; but the result was the same, and my top lip looked like a cornfield in late September before the stubble is ploughed under. And shaving twice is like being burned at the stake; the operation is seldom repeated on the same subject.

Since paying this terrible tribute to my vanity I have felt more than a little sorry for Antony, who, we are told by Enobarbus, was "barber'd ten times o'er" before calling on Cleopatra. Let us see how it was done. I suppose that even Antony, the demi-Atlas of this earth, could stand having his hair cut but twice at one sitting; and two shaves must have been about the limit of Roman endurance. That makes four barberings, leaving six yet unaccounted for. Well, we will have him twice singed; and after two hair-cuts this would be painful enough for the most painstaking lover. Next he shall have two shampoos, to alleviate the agony of his smoking poll. That leaves us with two tortures still unadministered. Maybe he went to a high-class barber's, the Roman equivalent for our perruquier, where corn-cutting was a side line of the business; and for the last operation we will assume he bought a bottle of brilliantine. This is a rather shabby way out of a difficulty, I know, but those ten barberings had to be explained away somehow, and if the process has been painful for Antony, I have at least successfully vindicated Shakespeare.

But imagine Antony with corns! Pursuing the frightful vision, we reel at the thought of a Cleopatra with chapped hands and a Caesar limping with an in-growing toenail.

We all grudge the time we spend at the barber's. It is so much sheer waste; to which is added the discomfort of sitting in a chair far too like a dentist's, and having our features mauled and pulled and twisted and pinched by a man who asks us questions which to answer would mean a severed jugular vein. Barbers and children are the only persons allowed to pull grown men's noses without having their own pulled in return. And both take full advantage of this privilege! Then there is the terror of the circular brush, which whirls across our heads like a mechanical road sweeper, and leaves us with every hair on end like quills upon the fretful porcupine.

Now comes the anointing process; and here is where our want of moral courage is displayed. He is a brave man who can persuade a barber, especially a Teuton, that his head does not want lubricating; that he has no desire to lard the lean earth when he ventures into the sun. Protest he never so loudly, the noisome unguents are rubbed into his scalp, and his hair is plastered down and polished as if for exhibition purposes. And when he goes into the street he feels that everybody is looking at him, and runs his hand nervously over his head and down the back of his neck. Now for a week onwards he must put a strip of paper inside his hat to prevent it dropping to his ears and extinguishing him altogether.

One of my earliest recollections is of sitting on the American-cloth settee at the barber's, my threepence clutched tightly in my hand, looking in wonderment down the dim perspective of the self-reflected mirrors, moving my head to see a whole regiment of heads move in chorus; and as I listened to the rasp of the razors, wondering if my innocent chin would ever discourse such excellent music. But when the necessity for shaving came, the anticipated pleasure gave place to horror. For never are we so completely at the mercy of our fellow man as when we lie back in the barber's chair, our hands and arms swathed in towels, our face besmeared with lather, while over us hovers the operator with his murderous blade. What if he went suddenly mad? What if, as he goes gingerly over the point of our jaw, somebody startled him and the razor slipped. Surely when he sees us thus helpless, our white throats invitingly stretched, he must be tempted? Small wonder that man has learned to shave himself. By-and-by there will come the super-man. He will cut his own hair, and life will have one trouble the less.

The Luncheon Hour

The hour at which we take the chief meal of the day marks much more effectually than salary or personal appearance our station in life. People who lunch at noon and dine at seven are a step higher in the social scale than we who dine at noon and have tea at home. Late dinner is the hall-mark of respectability. But it has its drawbacks. You learn at breakfast what to expect for dinner, and that is not good for you. Perhaps you hear the order given to the butcher for "a nice little loin of veal, not too fat," and all day long that nice little loin haunts you, and when on reaching home in the evening the odour of it assails your nostrils, loin of veal is the last thing you want. You have conceived a violent longing for liver and bacon, or something out of season.

But he who dines in the City at midday finds a spice of adventure in his meals. He does not know until within ten minutes of eating it what he is going to have. Even when he gets it he is not always sure. At twelve o'clock he feels hungry, and begins to think of dinner for the first time; and one o'clock sharp sees him at his accustomed table reading the menu. There are two ways of doing this. The first belongs to the man with the newspaper propped against the cruet. He orders the first joint on the list, and the first two vegetables, generally by indicating them with his finger; having done which he retires into his journal once more. To this man food is sustenance, necessarily only that he may live, and he takes no pleasure in what he eats. The second method is that of the epicure. He holds the menu up, reads it through carefully, glances over its top at what the man opposite has; pieces the dishes together in his mind, murmuring, almost as if he were tasting, the resulting combination; and finally gives his order with the air of a man who has done a good thing and done it well.

We Londoners have not yet mastered the art of eating out of doors. Even when we picnic in the country there is a shamefaced air about us, as if we were in deadly fear of being discovered. In town a few adventurous spirits, messenger boys and stockbrokers' clerks, eat while walking along, but it is not a success. In this connection it is worth noting that although I may walk through the City munching an apple or gesticulating with a half-stripped banana, I may not eat mutton chops, even cold ones, in the street. Whatever we may be at table, on the public highway we must be vegetarians.

The only man who can eat meat in the street and not lose his dignity is the navvy. He sits on a pile of macadam with but a scaffold pole between him and death by motor-bus, and frizzles his steak over a coke fire built in a pail, afterwards using his thumb and a hunk of bread for a plate. And who, catching a whiff of his fried onions, has not envied him? Truly, navvying has its compensations, for I may not eat onions. Consequently I am very fond of them, pickled. There is a sweet, tingling sensation, a kind of mental pins-and-needles about the flavour of a pickled onion; an exquisite clarity and sharpness like to the higher notes of a violin. You carry the delicately-veined sphere to your mouth and driving your teeth through its outer layers (the glory of that crunch, too!), your body thrills, your lips pucker, and the tears spring unbidden to your eyes. No other vegetable has this privilege of making us cry. We cannot weep at a potato, still less at a turnip. Scientists will explain these tears away, mentioning in doing so the over secretion of the lachrymal fluid, but I know better!

Have you ever felt your eyes grow moist when looking at some lovely view? Have you ever listened to beautiful music and felt your cheek to be wet afterwards? Milton tells us of Pluto, that listening to the lyre of Orpheus the "iron tears" coursed down his cheeks. We cannot say why we weep; it is done unconsciously, and with no obvious cause. I think it is partly at our own inability to grasp, to fully appreciate what we are looking at or listening to. And it must be that in the case of the onion. Anyway, I like to think it is! Why, there are ten miles of white road in Surrey that I remember solely because of the onions I found at an inn at my journey's end. They had been a year in pickle, and were a rich brown! But this pleasure of the onion is shut to us. Our friends will not put up with it. Society has said that onions are common, and there is an end to it. Yet I should not be surprised to hear that society ate onions in secret, or when on its holidays.

There are class distinctions even in vegetables and meats. If asparagus and truffles are the belted earls of the vegetable world, then onions and turnips are the mill-hands and agricultural labourers. Nobody has a good word to say for the onion; few will speak for the turnip. With meats, lamb represents the aristocracy, beef the prosperous middle class, mutton and pork the mediocrity of the menu. All this providing you give them their English names. Translate into French, and there is more liberty, equality, and fraternity in the matter. Sam Weller is, I think, the only man who has ever attempted to immortalise boiled mutton "with the usual trimmings"; and pork, roast pork, has had but one sponsor since it was marvellously discovered by Bo-bo and his father Ho-ti.

As a boy the choice of my dining place was always a matter for deep thought. During the morning I had been sent on perhaps four or five errands, journeys to banks and other offices; and each of these meant a bun or a "stone ginger" on the way back. Consequently by dinner-time my funds were reduced to twopence, and the provision of a satisfying meal with such a limited capital required careful planning. Two bananas and the largest bath bun in the E.C. district were the usual result of my deliberations. Armed with these I would dine surreptitiously in the Guildhall, pretending to read the lengthy inscriptions on the monuments there, meanwhile artfully conveying pieces of bun from my pocket to my mouth. What was left, and it was not much, the pigeons outside had. The next course was the mural paintings in the Royal Exchange. Dessert on the first three days of the week was an apple; on the other three an organ recital or a walk across London-bridge. But when I arrived home in the evening! Then Lucullus dined with Lucullus while the family looked on and wondered. They also asked questions about the disposal of my dinner-money, but my mouth was invariably full.

Now that these days are past, and most of us have been through them, we can look back to them and laugh. Yet for some this menu has served in after years, and then it is not a matter for jest.

Reading at Table

I suppose when one is married one does not read at meal times. I have yet to find out whether one would like to. It is considered, I believe, to be something of an insult to one's table companions; whereas it is more in the nature of a compliment to their good sense. Seated opposite to a fatuous ass, I cannot read. He does not want to, and therefore he talks—the last refuge of the vacant mind. He talks and talks at inordinate length about nothing whatever, and I have to grunt between mouthfuls, hurry my meal, and get indigestion.

But given a sensible table companion, I can take a bite and a page while he gets through a page and a bite; and each enjoys his meal, slowly and deliberately; secure in the knowledge that the other has done likewise.

Perhaps one will look up with a "Listen to this," and read a paragraph aloud; while the other will nod approval, and return to his book, himself to light on a dainty morsel worth sharing.

For all good conversation comes from books, and most of it is about books. And why should a book or paper be forbidden at table? We may read and smoke, read and drink, and (though this is not easy) read and walk; why should we not read and eat?

With me, reading at meals began at home. In the beginning there were nearly a hundred rules governing our conduct at table. We were not to eat too quickly, nor too slowly, nor too greedily, nor too daintily, nor put too much in our mouths at once, nor talk (think of that!), nor scrape with our feet on the rungs of the chairs, nor drink more than one glass of water, nor—. But the others were all the same. Normally about three of these rules were obeyed, excepting when

Aunt Emma was visiting us. Aunt Emma had views on children, but no children; as is the way of aunts who pay visits.

When she took the foot of the table there was nothing left but to stare at each other across the cloth, bite patterns in our bread and butter like the cave men's drawings of primitive horses; and nudge each other, suppressing, at the risk of choking, the consequent giggles. You see, we were very badly brought up; Aunt Emma said so. When she was not there we wrote our names on our plates with golden syrup, guiding the thin stream as it trickled from the spoon; or each counted the nuts on the top of the other's cake and squabbled about them. Or it may be, if it were fine and the evenings long, we sat and munched and munched as hurriedly as possible, slowing down when mother looked; and then, as at a given signal, gabbled full speed to "make us truly thankful," and bolted for the garden. As Aunt Emma said, we were very badly brought up; not like the children of her day. Smug little prigs!

It was the benevolent family doctor, I believe, who recommended a book at meals when there were no visitors. (He always gave us a shilling when we were ill, and though I once thought this was a kind of consolation prize, I now believe it to have been more in the nature of a thank-offering.) So we were allowed to read henceforward, and the silence at the tea-table was enormous. I have an old "Twenty Thousand Leagues Under the Sea" and a "Coral Island," in which I still find toast crumbs. Both are tea be-dropped, scarred with greasy thumb-marks, and every page in its time has been turned down at the corner.

Of course, grown-ups could always read at table if they wished. They were not supposed to obey rules, only to make them.

The books which one can read at mealtimes are few. Newspapers and letters are necessarily the only possible breakfast literature; and, by the way, this is the only fit time for the telling of last night's dreams. At any other meal they might be believed in, but at breakfast never. Dreams at supper have before now proved fatal.

Dinner, of course, calls for the undivided attention of the diner. It is next to impossible to dawdle over dinner—to do anything, in fact, but eat. It is too serious a business. The nature of the food and the implements used preclude the idea of reading. A loaded fork requires careful manipulation, or accidents may happen.

At lunch, the remainder of the newspaper and a page from one of the heavier weeklies will suffice. It is at the tea-table that mealtime reading becomes almost a necessity. With a little careful steering of the cup I can dip into and enjoy Addison, his "Spectator," Boswell, Elia, Hazlitt, Pepys. These are the tea-table gossips; these want the tinkle of the spoons.

But best of all is a good collection of letters. How people talked scandal before Thomas Garway opened his tea shop off Cornhill I cannot think. Scandal at lunch is out of place; still more so at breakfast. Tea, I think, must possess some property by which it engenders in the mind of the drinker a more than polite interest in the affairs of his neighbour. Curiosity flourishes in it, and that is why at tea time I prefer to pry into things which, although intensely interesting (as is all scandal), do not concern me. I can read Lamb's notes (and some of these were surely never meant for the vulgar eye), Sydney Smith's charming pen-chats to his daughter, Swift to Stella, and Carlyle to his friends. I can lift the curtain and peep into the secret places of the lives of these and other great souls; can meddle unabashed with another's domestic trifles, and read things about the dead which I could not bear to be told about the living.

A volume of letters laid at the left-hand side of my plate, or propped against the sugar-bowl, can be opened anywhere. There is no plot, no need for order in reading; and if, while both your hands are employed, the pages turn of themselves, why, even let them. This applies to no other reading matter. A book-mark is a superfluity with a volume of letters; tea and toast are necessaries.

Of Uncles

Give the matter thought, and you will find that uncles are really very important people indeed. Parents are every-day occurrences; uncles come from towns in the Midlands, from farms in Sussex, even from wonderful cities in America. Where other people "just drop in," uncles pay visits; which means, at the very least, staying to tea, and calling "good-night" up the stairs when we are undressing.

Again, it is always an uncle who has been to sea, who ran away from home, who was in the great earthquake, who went to Japan and made a fortune. Fathers never do these things, or if they do, they never tell; whereas the right sort of uncle will rattle off adventure after adventure, story after story; every fresh telling varying not one jot from the previous version.

And that is of all things the most important. To be a successful uncle you must have a good memory, and tell every story, true or fairy, exactly as you have told it before; neither adding to nor taking from the particulars, even in the interests of truth or scientific accuracy. You can try this with your nieces. Substitute a carrot for Cinderella's pumpkin; or, a less drastic change, a golden slipper for her glass one; you will be gently reproved and corrected. Persist in your vandalism and you produce tears.

Uncles, if they like, and they mostly do, can be of the greatest service to their nephews and nieces; especially their nephews. On warm summer evenings, and there really are such evenings, they will bowl for one by the hour; but fathers get tired after about a dozen slow lobs. Then Uncle Jim—nearly everybody has an Uncle Jim; in fact, I believe there are more Uncle Jims than ordinary Jims—Uncle Jim can make a ball break just where he likes, and once bowled Richardson at

95

the nets. He could have played for his county had he had more time. For the younger folks he can do any amount of tricks with folded paper; make cocked hats into boats and boats into fishes' heads that work their jaws. He can spin pennies, and keep them spinning, six at a time; and he doesn't say "bother" when you ask him to make a bunny with your handkerchief. He will play marbles or "Snap" as readily and enthusiastically as football or golf; and he plays them all equally well. Uncle Jim is an uncle worth having.

And then, of course (but this is quite a secondary consideration), uncles bring us things, and always the right things; just the book we have been wanting, just the very foreign stamp that will make our Heligoland page complete. As we get older, the choice of gift is left with us, and we are then initiated into the mysteries of the postal order. This amount of confidence in us is peculiar to our uncles; no one else will let us spend more than a penny without extending a firm guiding hand. Certainly, uncles are by far the best relations to have.

Consider grandfathers! They cannot run, and they must not be worried, and boys never played cricket or football in their day. Then, you must understand, children were kept in their proper place and taught to be seen and not heard, and all that sort of rot. That is when they are particularly grumpy; when they sit by the fire in the only really comfortable chair, with one foot resting on a hassock, and groan at intervals. In their lighter moments they are content to make glaring errors in a chap's age, talking about tops and hoops when he has turned fifteen; and to mix the batting and bowling averages in a most disheartening manner.

Moreover, we may not run into grandfather's bedroom in the morning, and climb all over him; and play "Little Princes in the Tower" with the pillows, like the illustrations in the big Shakespeare on the sideboard. Grandfathers are too fragile for children. But uncles— One can do anything with a decent uncle; pull his moustache, even his nose, turn out his pockets, wind his watch, ruffle his hair. Any one of these things tried on a grandfather, especially when his foot is resting on a hassock, means early bed.

Nor are cousins of much use. Either they are of about our own age, in which case they are liable to fight; or they are eighteen, despising small boys and garden cricket with a soft ball. They seldom take us to the theatre, and when they do, try hard to look as if we did not belong to them. But uncles will go with us even to a circus (there are one or two still left in England), and laugh at the ringmaster's discomfiture as loudly as we do. They do not mind what they do, or who sees them doing it. They know, better than anybody, that it is impossible to be dignified and happy at the same time. It is always an uncle who lends his handkerchief to Mr. Devant for his second trick; no cousin could do this.

Many fathers are uncles as well, and it is remarkable that from the point of view of those to whom they are uncles, they are as good as every other uncle. The best of uncles is no more than an ordinary father when he is at home. The reason of this is that when people go visiting they leave a part of themselves at home, and drop a few of their years. Thus an ordinary father can be quite a jolly old uncle.

I pity the boy with no uncles. He, indeed, misses many of youth's pleasures; with no Uncle Walter to come up for the pantomimes; no Uncle Davy to send him strings of horse-chestnuts in October; no Uncle Jim to stay week-ends and instruct him in the art of rabbit feeding and the bowling of "googlies."

Now, all this is rather hard on fathers, but they will understand. When young, we take no thought of ordinary days. Life then is composed of holidays; the blanks between which are eternities. And uncles are holidays; when they come they have time to spare.

Later on, as we grow up, we find our uncles slipping away from us, one by one; and presently we cease to be nephews, and soon are uncles ourselves. And if we have been good nephews, and remember our uncles, we shall be good uncles, and remember our nephews.

Slippers

To the man who loves his household gods the operation known as "clearing out" is a terrible business. One day (it generally happens on a bright spring morning) he tells himself he will have a "clear out" and dispose of some of his old rubbish. So he starts on the mantel-shelf, and seldom gets any further. For he finds that the curled and grimy photographs there are more than mere photographs; that he needs must keep every one of his rank, chipped briars, although they will never be smoked again. As of the smaller items, so is this true of old jackets. The man who can throw away an old jacket, a jacket he has worked and made holiday in—such a man is without form and void. For a good jacket never gets so old that it cannot be worn. Following this rule, by the time a man is forty he will have accumulated something like two dozen old jackets, which he cannot wear out of doors and must not give away. This, however, is a problem which every man must solve for himself or leave to his wife.

Strong as is my aversion to parting with a left-off jacket, still more strong is my attachment to my slippers. But the pair I have now are condemned; for they are most comfortingly disreputable. Split and torn and broken, they will hardly hang together; and in addition to ruining my socks, they make me fall upstairs. However, since they must be renounced, I have managed to assure them a fitting end. They shall not be given to the dustman or the jobbing gardener (both of whom would doubtless refuse the gift as having no realisable value). They are to be burnt, with all proper ceremony, on the very next washing day; and in their death they shall kindle a purging fire for the cleansing of my more intimate garments.

So I must get new slippers, since they cannot be bought second-hand. Hats, coats, and boots all come in due time to the old clothes mart, but when did you see a pair of old slippers thus pining for ownership? It has been said that no good work was ever done in slippers, but remarks like that are easy to make. For instance, no good cricket was ever played in evening dress. Slippers are not meant for work, and no good loafing has ever been done out of them. The majority of the men who have enriched the world with the fruits of their genius never wore slippers, excepting always the gentler poets, the dreamers. To do good practical work it is necessary that one should be a little uncomfortable. That is why bank clerks and chartered accountants are obliged to wear stiff collars. Comfort is fatal to energy, and slippers are the emblem of comfort, the last word in luxurious ease. When you are sitting in an armchair boots are absurd. They take you all too easily back to work, to pavements and closing prices and the scramble for bread. Their weight holds you down, prevents your rising above the silly, sordid world. Armchairs and boots can no more be reconciled than silk hats and walking tours. Boots are civilisation's great failure. You can send a birthday greeting round the world in a few hours, but you cannot buy a pair of boots that do not hurt you somewhere while they are new.

Wars are planned by men in boots; trusts, corners, robberies, murders are thought out by men with heavily-shod, firmly-planted feet. It is next to impossible to plan a bad deed or think a wicked thought with your feet in slippers. There are exceptions, and no doubt murders have been arranged by men in armchairs and wearing slippers, but I doubt if they were great successes. It is not that slippers make a man gentle. You may live in slippers and be a villain, but, I think, not so downright a villain as you might have been had you stuck to hob-nailed boots.

Some poetry is obviously born of slippers. I would suggest that the "Ode to a Nightingale" was written on a warm, heavy-scented evening, in a garden between high yew hedges, the poet pacing the dewy lawn in his slippers. It could hardly have been otherwise. Arguing along the same lines, we must arrive at the conclusion that the "Charge of the Light Brigade" was penned in top boots and spurs.

Again, had Omar trodden his strip of herbage in spring-sides would there have been the "Rubaiyat"? To come to prose, could Lamb have written of, say, Sarah Battle and Whist had he worn patent leathers? "A clear fire, a clean hearth, and the rigour of the game." The opening sentence calls for slippers.

There is no doubt that the best solid thinking is done in boots; while the finest dreams, the tenderest thoughts, are encouraged by slippers. Perhaps the reason for this lies in some sympathetic connection between our toes and the gentler side of our brains. You may cut a finger or knock your knee-cap, and, apart from the actual physical pain, you are not much perturbed. Yet one little corn, or the stubbing of a toe against the washing-stand, and your peace of mind is temporarily wrecked. The effect is to irritate where an injury to another part of the body would merely hurt. Free your feet from their leathern confines, those pinching, materialistic boots, and let them nestle at their ease, while you, unfettered, dream dreams and twiddle your toes. Clamp your feet tightly in neat's leather and you compile dictionaries, calculate stresses and strains, build bridges, and fight battles.

Slippers should be of carpet. Those imitation leather things that other people buy for us are but miserable hypocrites, neither fish nor fowl, nor boot nor slipper, but aspiring to be both. Slippers should be of carpet, gaudy in red, green, blue, and brown; startling and ugly, but wondrous relieving after the sombre monotony of boots. Out of doors we are a sober suited people, choosing our ties carefully that they shall not offend, dressing largely in black, or compromising with cowardly greys and browns and blues. But in the privacy of our own homes, where we can really do as we like, our pyjamas would put a rainbow to shame and our carpet slippers are kaleidoscopic.

For absolute comfort they should be three sizes too large. This is true of all clothes, but possible only with slippers. They should be big enough to make lifting the feet in walking an impossibility. The shuffle of the carpet slipper wearer, the steady, even glide—these are not the least soothing of their properties.

But they are seductive things. No matter what your plans for the evening may be, whether you meant to plant out some seedlings, nail up the creeper, or mend the trellis work; once you stand in your slippers your plans go for naught. If you do not actually drop into a chair and a book, the most you will rise to is a walk round the garden, making more plans for to-morrow evening, or next month, or next year.

The Comforter

Lately I have been sleeping badly; and twice within a week daylight has crawled over the chimney-pots and into the bedroom to find me still awake. On each of these mornings I have leaned from my window to listen to a blackbird who sits and plays his whistle in our sycamore. (It is really only a Dicky-bird tree.)

The thing is so wonderful, because that poor starved tree is the only vegetation in my world. All the rest is bricks and mortar and slates; beneath which, when I lie awake, I hear the steady breathing of thousands of people, with sometimes a sigh here and there. But that is between one and two of the morning. Later comes my blackbird to sing to me and chase away the bogies of the night. I have often wondered why he comes here. There are no gardens, no worms or slugs, nothing to interest him. I like to think it is for me he comes, to cheer me until the world is awake, and work takes my thoughts from myself. Maybe it is an order. Perhaps there are other blackbirds near crowded hives, hospitals, and the like, piping to other tortured souls. But that, I suppose, is a silly fancy.

Mine comes with the dawn, before the air is sullied with the fumes of your million eggs and bacon; and he goes just as soon as the first chimney begins to smoke. Meanwhile I lie quietly in my bed and think of June evenings, and dark shrubberies, and long shadows on the grass. I am grateful to my blackbird, and wish heartily I might tell him so. If I knew how to make him understand, I would get him some fat worms and ripe berries and put them where he would find them. Yet I have an idea that he knows; else why should he come to sing to me morning after morning? Also, I wonder whence he comes. I like to imagine his little cradle as hung away in some fine elm-hidden rectory garden, or subtly poised in a tangle of hazel and honeysuckle, with a brook near by. If that is so, he must get up very early, for there is no honeysuckle within many miles of my sycamore. In spite of the chimney-pots, his song is that same sweet pipe, that same mellow flute note heard at twilight in a Devon combe or in the cool shade of a Sussex hanger.

Last Sunday I heard him, and for a time he comforted me, until the devil of discontent took possession of my soul. Then I thought to follow him, to learn what he could see in this grey world to make him so light-hearted. So, creeping from the house, I took train to the little hills, and until dark followed my quest along the Pilgrims' Way.

You must know how this highway runs high along the roof of a fair country, between fir trees and blue distances, close up under the sky; and on my Sunday there was no other soul in all England that wished to go along the Pilgrims' Way. So I shared it with my blackbird until I came to Newland's Corner. Here the trees are drawn aside, and suddenly, from the sun-splashed twilight of the woods, you are thrust into the open again, among the clouds, to stare half across the world and nearly to the sea. Here it was I met a nut-brown maid astride a ridiculously fat donkey. She was fifteen years of age, she told me, and her father sold roots and plants, and mended chair-bottoms all up and down England. She was not a real gipsy, not a Boswell or a Lovell; but her little brother over there in the wood had six fingers on each hand—or, rather, five fingers and a thumb. She charged me twopence for this information, and with her blessing I followed my blackbird along the road to Guildford.

By Martha's Chapel, where again I had the earth to myself, I went on my knees to the violets, like fragments of a fallen sky, while overhead the bird chuckled at this further foolishness. Later, as I waited for the train, I heard him laughing in the stationmaster's garden; and I think he must have heard me singing. For he piped: "I did it. I did it. Cheer up! Come again. I did it!"

In the train I shared a carriage with three other men, each with dusty boots, and each wearing a faded wild flower of some kind in his buttonhole. A girl stood on the platform, smiling into our carriage, and one of the men was leaning through the window to say good-bye to her.

"Cheer up. Cheer up!" piped my blackbird. "Good-bye," said the man; "I'll be down again to-morrow week." You should have heard my blackbird laugh.

Then the man leaned further through the window and kissed the girl, and bumped his head when he came in again; and the train slid out of the station. So the man who had bumped his head rubbed the place and hummed a tune to show that he had not kissed the girl; and five minutes later he was asleep in a corner seat, with a silly smile on his face, so that I knew my blackbird ordered his dreams.

The others gazed out of the window at the fading picture that flashed by, and presently one drew forth a pocket diary.

"One, two, three, four"—up to eight he counted slowly. Then he tried it again as if he would make it less, but with the same result.

"Are you going away in July, then?" asked his friend; and I fancied I heard that blackbird shout through the open window. But I must have been mistaken, because it was nearly dark; and a thin sickle of light showed where the moon hung, a weak usurper on the sun's cold throne.

At a little station higher up the line (and I remember the whiff of hawthorn that came when the door was opened) a fat man with a bag of golf clubs got in; and, on the strength of a borrowed match, struck up a conversation, in which he wondered how the devil the markets would open on the morrow.

So I take it my blackbird was at home, and asleep.

The Time Machine

Working Backwards.

It was probably a prehistoric labourer who first thought to measure time; a hairy man sitting tailor-wise under a thorn bush, chipping flints. Maybe he spaced the tide marks on a river's bank, or marked the crawling shadow of a tree; and by these signs made out the first time sheet, scrawled on a scrap of birch bark with a sheep's tooth.

Since then the thing has become a mania with us, and we have learned to chop our lives into years, our years into months and weeks and days, our days into hours and minutes; and these last, just to show our cleverness, we have minced into seconds and fractions of seconds. The consequence is that clocks tick.

But this must not be thought about; for if you sit in your arm chair, alone, and listen to the clock it says, "Nearer, nearer, nearer, nearer"; and at six minutes to the hour it makes a little choking noise in its throat as if it were going to say something.

They are awful things, ticking clocks; carpenters at work, with little, little hammers, making coffins.

When we record the passing of time, we do but mark the passing of ourselves. The clocks tick and strike, the leaves fall from the calendar, one by one, stealthily, until the year is bare. Then we buy a new calendar, and say we are a year older. That alone shows the absurdity of it all, for who is there that is really a year older for having lived another 365 days? Counting mile-stones is a profitless way of spending a journey.

The truth is that we are just as young as we feel. To-day, if it be fine, we are twenty-four, and the birth certificate in the top drawer lies with its story of 1876; the registrar was drunk. We are as young as we feel. This must be true because it is so beautiful, and withal so necessary to life. Once realise that you are forty and think of all that forty means, and you are undone.

We are as young as we feel. Do you not remember schoolboys of thirty, wearing goggles, and eternally swotting French which was to be useful to them in business, but never was? Do you not know of boys of forty and fifty, young oldsters; ready for anything from garden cricket to bears on the landing?

On 10 April there is a blue sky, with brave sailing clouds and a fair wind, and you are twenty-eight. On the 11th, certain people go to the trouble of pointing out that you are forty-one. Some even write to you about it—yes, and congratulate you on it.

As if you had not been trying for weeks to forget it.

Then, for a few days perhaps, you walk soberly to the station, and wonder at lunch time whether you ought to eat certain things. But with fair luck and a good liver you will get your age down to thirty in a fortnight, and if the weather holds to twenty-eight eventually.

But there are times other than birthdays when the years pile suddenly upon our shoulders, and on these occasions the load falls the heavier. It was thus that I was visited but a few days ago. Previously I had spent life enjoying to-day and looking forward to to-morrow; when of a sudden my eyes were turned to yesterday; to a yesterday which I, living for the minute, had long forgotten. And in a little I was old, so old.

It was a wet afternoon, and I could not find the book for my mood. So after wandering up and down the shelves for half an hour I relinquished the idea of reading, and started on that awful business, "clearing up." For most of us this means turning out cupboards and putting the things back again, if anything a trifle more higgledy-piggledy than they were before. It is a melancholy occupation, and you are almost certain to cry when you do it; for you will come upon an odd skate, a pair of dumb-bells, or the hat you were married in; all relics of the hopeless, helpless, resurrected past.

It was an old black box that gave up the dry bones of my youth; a cricket bat, sprung; a wicket-keeping glove; a fishing-rod, all but the top joint and the winch; and some other such things, which, had I been wise, I should have burned or given away years ago. Of course, there were books; the sort that no respectable boy would be seen reading, but which he would read all the same; and it was amongst these that I found my old Simpson's Euclid, a pedagogue fallen among thieves, with a horrible date on the fly leaf, and one corner mildewed.

The axioms and postulates were missing, but Prop. V. was still there; that wicked old triangle, that terrible structure on which a million generations of boys have been tied and flogged.

I sat on the box and ran over the problem, but could no more understand it than I could in those green years when it absorbed my half holidays. Yet I found myself as ready as ever to take the author's word for it that the angles on the other side of the base are equal. After all, what does it matter if they are not?

There is more than mere Euclid on that page to puzzle me. For instance, the triangle ABC has been embellished with two eyes, a nose and a mouth; and the bisecting lines BG and CF tricked out to resemble a passable collar and tie. Obviously this stood for somebody, but for whom I cannot be certain. It may have been meant for the French master; there is something of a likeness. And his memory is certainly worth perpetuating, for he was, I believe, the only French master in England whose nickname was not "Froggy." We called him "Snail-broth"; and in moments of extreme emotion he would retaliate with "Costermongers" and "Pigs," which we certainly were; and some rather advanced idioms, which I am not sure about.

Or it may have been intended for "Granny," who took us in mathematics and was mad on fungi. His practice was to set a problem to keep us quiet, and spend the rest of his two hours dissecting loathsome and smelly little toadstools.

Overleaf, where the plot of the proposition begins to get exciting (wherefore these triangles are equal, and their remaining angles each to each, to which the equal sides are opposite), I find a minute note in the margin which says, "Boffin, 1½d." Boffin, I remember, was the red-haired son of the Rev. Bryn Scones, and he was fat and pimply, which accounted for his nickname. I cannot see the connection now, but I know there was one. I wonder whether I lent Boffin three-ha'pence, or borrowed that sum from him. As a rule, neither was possible.

It is by looking back at our youth that we realise our years, and when I rose from that box I felt nearly grey.

But I would rather grow old suddenly, with a generous draught from the flagon of life, than slowly, in little sips, to the ticking of a clock.

He who does this last will one day find the measure empty, and his thirst unslaked.

Writing Home

Lying in a hollow I had scooped in the shingle little more than a dozen feet from the bubbling fringe of the last wave, I laboriously scribbled these words, and then lay back to think about them.

The last postcard from home, two days ago, had said, "Write soon," and I could not understand their desire for letters. Why should they, still catching the 8.30 every morning, still kicking against London's bricks and mortar; why should they want to know of my goings and comings? My letters, scanty as they were, could but serve to make their shackles the heavier. Yet there must be something akin to pleasure in this self-torture; the pleasure of a hungry man staring through a pastry-cook's window; of the convict snuffing the breeze through his high grating.

I think it is unkind to write home when making holiday; almost as unkind as for those at home to expect letters from you. They want to know what you are doing, forsooth! They want nothing of the kind. Think how every word of what you write must sting them as they read your scribble in the lapses of their day's work.

"Yesterday we bathed early." Bathed, in fact, just as they were struggling for their everlasting train; plunging into a mob of their fellows; all brushed and be-collared into employable respectability; scurrying to their appointed places with no thoughts but of 6 p.m. and pay day. This while I, with a day of sixteen full free hours before me, ran laughing into the marbled waves, and fought the waters with the new-found strength of ten.

"And later, walked across the Downs, through Fox Hole to Wilmington." Thus is dismissed that glorious tramp up and over the close bit slopes, all lit and darkened by the hurry of the clouds; the halt at the shepherd's cottage, where in mellow cider we drank to the hour-old babe squalling upstairs; the long rest on the hill-top amongst the gorse and the rabbits; and the tired but tuneful plod back to food and sleep.

But it would be cruel to tell them this, and also it would take too long. Their imaginations will surely supply the details, to the unrest of their souls. Yet it is hardly consideration which is at the bottom of these curt notes; there is a deal of laziness in it. My last letter home took two of us nearly a day to write. My nearest neighbour, you must know, was Eastwick, the coastguard, and he was a mile away. But on Tuesday morning Fate sent him down to our bungalow with two cabbages; so I borrowed his jack knife and sharpened two pencils while he told me all about what he called "foreign parts" and the Anthropophagi, and sea serpents, and burning ghats, and women. All I remember of the conversation is that Bombay stinks worse than Calcutta, and "bein' a coastguard is like puttin' that there sea-gull in a paper bag. Walk up and down the cliff, meet the man from the next station, and dig the garden. That's bein' a coastguard. What does a first-class petty want with diggin' taters?"

By the time Mr. Eastwick had finished I had sharpened the pencils, and he accordingly took his jack knife back with him. I thought about him and his troubles for about half a pipe; and then settled down to think what to put in my letter. You see there was no excuse, no way out at all. Paper and envelopes were by my side, and both my pencils were beautifully sharpened. I began to wish Eastwick had stopped away.

Presently I was inspired. "Dear Everybody," I wrote; "The weather so far has been lovely"; then lay back and laughed into the blue.

Before me the sea played sleepily with the pebbles; behind the Downs rose and fell in massy curves, as if the earth breathed deeply. Overhead a gull tacked about and about, and broke the monotonous sky into life. How could I tell them all this? Enough that it was mine and not theirs; mine to absorb and enjoy, but not to tell about.

"What can I say next?" I asked.

"Tell 'em about the hours we keep," suggested my companion. "That ought to be good for half a page."

So I told them of our goings and comings to the extent of half a page. Then I put a stone on the letter and ran into the sea. There I got another idea worth quite ten lines and scampered back to make a note of it. In the afternoon we took the still unfinished letter to the top of the cliff, and in the intervals of smoking and throwing stones at a thistle head, I managed to turn out another two pages. Towards the end, I am afraid, the writing was very large. For, lying on the top of a cliff, all that is of moment is the present, and a tiny bit of the future; about as far as mid-day to-morrow. Then I hope to walk up the hill to Eastwick's cottage and borrow his razor if he is not using it. To recount what we did yesterday I told myself, would be tedious to myself and painful to my audience; and further I was not at all sure what it was we did.

One day, I remember, we took a bagful of bread and cheese, and four bottles of ginger beer, baled out the Moss Rose, and took her six miles up the little river; now punting her, now rowing, now letting the tide have its way. Coming back we rigged up a jury mast and sail with the help of two oars and a mackintosh, and sped along luxuriously at a good three miles an hour. Now, how can I tell them that? It is impossible that these holiday letters should be as acceptable as the recipients would have us believe. And I am certain that the writers get little pleasure from them. Hence the picture post-card.

When the letter was at last written, Eastwick came down the hill in response to the semaphoring of a bathing costume on a broom handle, and took it four miles to post. I think his views on holiday letters are very like my own.

Some Ancestors

After the destruction of the case of stuffed birds (Uncle Jack had been showing us how Indian jugglers climb up invisible ropes), the album was no longer required as a pedestal, and soon drifted into the lumber-room with the old picture frames, the History of England in fifty parts, unbound, and the flowerpots.

I have no doubt that you remember the stuffed birds—parrakeets from the Indies, a bullfinch from a Hertfordshire lane, two or three love-birds, and a sparrow-hawk—grouped on a piece of seaweed-covered rock, in attitudes of brotherly love, with a fixed, feeding-time glare in their frozen eyes.

You will remember the album also; its brass clasp with which you were not to fiddle; its big gilt-edged pages, their oval and oblong holes all festooned with gay blossoms. If you had such an album, and if you were normally wicked children, it was a wet afternoon's amusement to laugh and poke fun at the queer little aunts and uncles and cousins of a generation ago preserved within the covers of your book.

Eked out with hymns in the sitting-room, our album was the one relaxation in the long, long hours between morning service and bedtime at Aunt Julia's.

Looking through the faded cartes de visite, the first thing that strikes me is that all my aunts were once young. That was certainly before they entered my world, and, I suppose, before they entered aunthood.

Some of them are quite small girls, wearing hoops, and stockings with horizontal lines running round them, like peppermint-rock. Aunt Julia herself is there, wearing a tiny straw hat over one eye, and holding an absurd basket in one hand, while with the other she pretends to open a practicable gate. There is a studied coyness about her, a stiff, five-second-exposure smile, with a something uncomfortable behind it, as if she were wearing her best clothes for the first time, as was probably the case.

But consider Aunt Julia these days. She is ample and beaded, and she has no need of hoops, even were they fashionable. Neither is there anything coy about her, unless it be her daughters.

It was our custom on long evenings, when the grown-ups were out of the way, to weave romantic stories round the folk in our album; dramatic rescues of simpering females by heroic uncles, whom we afterwards married to each other, recklessly, and without regard to kindred or affinity.

Such a hero was Uncle Charles, who in the picture before me stands beside a rich plush curtain, holding in one hand a rough-coated high hat, and wearing trousers of a pattern wonderful to behold. Now, Uncle Charles had but one leg, his missing limb being replaced by a timber prop.

This circumstance provided us with endless realms of gold, romances in which Uncle Charles was always the central figure, laying about him with a will. But our inventive faculties received a rude shock when cautious inquiries discovered the fact that the missing leg was removed in a hospital at South Shields as the result of a most commonplace accident.

One of us, I know, was moved to tears when assured that this was the truth of the matter. It was finally decided by a committee of four, sitting in the tool-shed on a wet day, that this account of Uncle Charles's loss should be ruled out of order, and an exciting time was spent in suggesting substitutes.

A Red Indian theory was rejected on the ground that no respectable Blackfoot would remove a man's leg, scalps being notoriously the only trophies collected by those gentlemen.

The hero of the "Ballad of Chevy Chase" attracted us, because, as you know,

> When his legs were smitten off
> He fought upon his stumps.

But Uncle Charles still had one leg left, so we agreed that the other was removed in the course of a desperate encounter with Chinese pirates off the Andamans.

Aunt Margaret is next, in a spacious crinoline, one hand resting negligently on a tall pedestal, the other dangling a beaded reticule. She was twenty-three when this photograph was taken; but we never saw her until she was white, and seventy. When I was older, and knew, I think I cried over Aunt Margaret a little; she had such a sweet face, a face to go with fireside armchairs and chubby babies, a face to which you would take your troubles. It seemed such a pity she should have died single. When I last saw her, she was sitting on a low stool before the fire, her little slippers on the fender, her tired eyes seeing nothing, her thin blue-veined hands mechanically working the embroidered bellows.

But more pathetic even than these disturbing relics are those pictures of fat little humans, seated half-dressed on hairy rugs (which must have been very uncomfortable), which pictures we are a little ashamed to learn are of ourselves. I say ashamed, because few men can look upon these pictures of their early selves and not think how much they have lost. When we sat on those rugs there was that in our eyes which must have abashed the photographer; innocence, wonderment, and not a little contempt for the bald lie about the little bird which he would have had us believe. Our later portraits have knowledge in their eyes, and craft and guile; and for these we pose shamelessly. The purpose of this must surely be to mislead the photographer. Ourselves we cannot deceive, our friends and relatives also know us.

Perhaps nobody gets nearer to the naked soul than the amateur, wandering at large with his film-charged camera and all-seeing eyes. He gets us when we are bathing, or falling from our bicycles, or swearing, or looking foolish, or merely imbecile; and he sends us prints of our noble selves in these ridiculous attitudes, libels all, of course.

Our grandfathers were spared this humiliation. Photography with them was not a pastime, but a serious business, requiring almost as much deliberation as matrimony, or buying a horse. Witness the studied grimness of their faces, the stiffness of their attitudes, practised, maybe, before the long glass in the wardrobe previous to setting out. And where the present-day amateur is content with a brick wall or a row of scarlet-runners by way of background, the gentleman who "took" grandfather bestowed great thought on this matter of properties—a heavy plush chair and a Bible for one over 50, a pedestal for the young buck of 25, and a gate or stile, with a small basket of flowers, for the ladies.

But we must be careful how we treat the matter of these old photographs. It is by no means a jest. For one day, if we be worthy, we may ourselves find a niche between the heavy covers of some family album, and help a future generation of nieces and nephews through a wet Sunday afternoon.

Can you not hear them? "Oh! Here's old Uncle So-and-so. What an absurd little person!"

Our Ship

"When our ship comes home—" I began.

"Poor old crock," said the Girl. "It's been so long coming that its provisions must have run out and the crew starved to death. I can see it, bobbing about somewhere, derelict, and covered with noisy gulls."

"When our ship comes home," I persisted, "I will buy us a cosy flat beside the park, easy for the theatres, and close to the Round Pond where the babies play.

"I will fill it with my own beloved books and pipes and pictures, and my fine full-bodied arm-chairs. It shall have big wood fires in winter, beside which you and I will sit. And you shall no longer squat on the fender and sew up the finger tips of your gloves.

"Instead, we shall dine at cheap and shabby little foreign restaurants in Old Compton-st., with stalls to follow."

"All very pretty, and all very selfish," said the Girl. "So far there's nothing of mine in your flat. Besides, flats are stuffy. They remind me of the time when I kept white mice. They only lack the wheel that you get inside and turn with your feet. And you have to have your garden on the window sill ... Now I've pricked my finger, and it's bled on the glove, and that's eight three-farthings gone smack."

I attended to the wound, which was not serious. "When our ship comes home," continued the Girl, "I mean to have a nice roomy Elizabethan house on the sunny side of a hill and near a wood. And I want cool lawns and long shadows, and big linen-cupboards, and a kitchen like a baronial hall, with bright dish covers for shields round the walls."

She took up the poker and stared into the fire.

"Then our ship must fall in with a rich Spanish galleon on its way home," I said. "For such a house in such a spot means a motor-car as well."

"Why 'a motor-car'?" she asked. "Why not a pretty little governess-car and a Shetland? They are very cheap"—a little doubtfully—"in the country, so I've heard."

"No," I insisted, "it will have to be a motor. There are very few shops on the sunny side of your hill, and you would want things. Then, supposing one night the children—" (here the Girl poked the fire very hard)—"supposing the children developed croup. Nearest doctor four miles, post-office six, and shut, and no vinegar in the house. What then?"

The Girl got up from the fender and sat on the floor.

"I resign," she said. "The Elizabethan house must have a motor with it. But did babies have croup in Elizabethan houses before motors were? And did they die?"

"The resident priest was usually something of a physician," I hazarded. "However, as you don't like my flat, and I see objections to your house on the hill, suppose we try again … I remember a picture I brought back in my mind's eye from somewhere, a fairly large house, one of those square-built, solid-looking structures, rather ugly outside, but full of fine rooms and warm red lights and hangings. It stood in its own grounds, and I went in to ask my road. I remember there was a terrace, with roses, and a statue of Pan; and an alley of clipped yews and box, leading to a shrubbery. I have always wanted a shrubbery."

The Girl shuddered. "Shrubberies mean big fat spiders, and cobwebs across your face. No! Shrubberies and yew walks are for the old folk to wander in. Give me roses, and bright beds of geraniums, and calceolarias. A lawn if you like, and a sundial that won't interfere with the croquet. But no shrubbery! Cypress, and yew, and box, and privet belong to cemeteries."

"Then we will say no more about the shrubbery," I said. "We will furnish this house, and then we'll move in. The drawing-room, of course, would have an Adam fireplace, with Diana at the chase in marble. There should be one real Morland, a Constable, an Old Crome (how the money runs away!), a Clausen, 'Mowing Bracken' would do, and some good china. Nothing decorates like good blue and white, you know.

"The furniture, of course, would be Adam, in warm walnut; but as Adam is nothing if it isn't uncomfortable, there would have to be two big armchairs, this and another."

"Dark red curtains in the winter," chimed in the Girl; "white and gold wallpaper, a maroon carpet, and a blue Persian kitten. And, oh! that oval mirror we saw in the Tottenham-court-rd."

"And I should sit smoking in the window seat (that's another thing I've always wanted), 'while you sat and played toccatas, stately at the clavichord.' Or would the dark red curtains prohibit my smoking?"

I don't think the Girl was listening; but I went on.

"But when we get this house, there must be one plebeian room tucked away somewhere, where I can stow the precious odds and ends I have accumulated and lived with so far. They might strike a jarring note if put in our beautiful drawing-room; but for a snuggery, twelve by sixteen, up three flights of stairs, there isn't their equal.

"There's my rocky old desk, for instance, and the little chipped God of Content that you gave me for a paper weight. And the Toby jug that I bought for fourpence, and the fretwork pipe rack that I made myself out of somebody else's cigar boxes.

"Then there's the reproductions of the 'Angelus,' and Rembrandt's 'Head of an Old Woman,' and the 'Laughing Cavalier,' and the grocer's almanack from home.

"Remember when I bought the back numbers of the 'World's Art Treasures,' sevenpenny numbers for twopence each; and we spent an evening discussing how they should be framed? And in the end, I stuck them on the walls with drawing pins.

"I want all those things in my one little room, with the sprung bat in the corner, and the bright pewter tankard on the desk."

"What do you think it will really be?" asked the Girl. "A flat in the Holloway-rd.?"

"Heaven preserve us from that," I said, devoutly. "But I really don't know. It may go to a little house down Chiswick way. Pomander-walk, perhaps."

"Half-way to fairyland! Just what I've been wanting," said the Girl. "Those big houses are so full of echoes."

The Awakening

The prongs of the fork rang on the frozen soil when the Girl first went gardening, sticking little dry twigs here and there round the border. With the thaw she spent another morning arranging entanglements of white cotton, weaving her intricate meshes from one twig to another. Clothes-lines for the fairies' washing day she called them; but that I knew well enough was not right. Fairies do not wear clothes; and, besides, they go to sleep all winter. The real object of the cotton was to keep the sparrows from the coming crocus-tops; and I, shaving by the window, watched these things and laughed derisively.

There never had been a summer, I pointed out, and there never would be. Such things existed only in books about the tropics. Here in our garden life was just alternate frost and thaw. For years we had stamped our feet and blown upon our fingers; and these stories of heat and sun were untrue.

I put some more coal on the fire, and stood on the hearthrug to draw it up.

Then for two days it drizzled and was warm. The brown earth seemed to breathe again, to stir in its sleep. The buds on the sycamore had each a glistening raindrop, like a silver berry, and as these slid down the twigs and into one another, they became too heavy and dropped to the ground.

Two mornings later the Girl, again pottering round the sodden waste, ran indoors crying that the earth had cracked. "There *is* going to be a summer," she said. "The earth has cracked, and there's a crocus peeping through. Come and see!"

There was, too! I looked closely into the tiny fissure, and saw the plucky green spear-point forcing its way through the yielding soil. All round the border there were cracks, and the Girl opened one or two with a hairpin to see if there really were crocuses below them. Altogether we found 27 coming flowers, and the Girl danced up and down the path.

"Don't be absurd," I said; "it happens every year."

"So does this!" said the Girl, and danced again.

Snow followed, and hung about for a week; London snow, all spotted with soot, and getting dirtier and dirtier; stopping the promising cracks in the garden, and freezing our young crocuses to death.

But presently a miracle happened, and now the garden is all lit with little candle flames that flicker in the wind. The crocuses have won their way to the light.

It all happened two nights ago. A warm rain had dripped all day from a smoky sky, until the earth looked as if it steamed. Hope was certainly dead in us, and even the Girl would not brave the depression outside to look for buds.

Yet in the morning there were the crocuses with their golden banners, and in the centre of one clump a scilla showed, like a fallen flake of a June sky. The bright blades of the hyacinths, too, were making a brave show, and down in their hearts I could see the ready buds climbing up to the coming sun.

On that morning, for the first time this year, I cleaned my boots while walking round the garden, and that is a good sign. I found little timorous leaves frilling the elderberry, and the buds on the sycamore were a brighter green. I do not think my boots have had such a polish for a long time. These buds, and blooms, and promises made me stick my chest out, and bustle about, and pick up stray twigs, and knock a nail in the trellis, and sweep the path, and whistle all the time; while through the open window came sounds of cups and saucers and snatches of song. Wonderful!

The next day was even better. Two more crocuses had put on their new clothes during the night, and the stirring of the sap was showing itself in all sorts of ways. Next door the chicken-house was getting a coat of green paint; while on the other side a man was cutting dahlia sticks for dahlias not yet planted out. When he saw me he looked a little foolish, but I helped him out by asking him if he had a little raffia to spare.

It was a mad day altogether. The Girl chased a robin out of the garden because he looked like a Christmas card, and twice I banged on the window to scare the sparrows. I love sparrows for their impudence; but I cannot stand their ingratitude. All the winter through we have spread crumbs abroad for them; they have had the waste from the canary's cage; and their water-bowl has been washed out and refilled daily. So to see them deliberately eating the hearts out of my crocuses, tearing the petals off to get at their sweet tit-bit, this makes me indignant.

And when I knock on the window, they fly just as far as the fence, where they sit and pass remarks about me until my back is turned again. Strewing crumbs is no good now, for no respectable sparrow will touch bread while there are sweet crocus petals about. Nor does the web of cotton worry the little vandals. I think they steal it for nesting purposes.

So we turned the cat into the garden. The cat's name is Tozzy Nim, and her favourite occupation is lying in a patch of sunlight. The garden was all sunlight this mad morning, and Tozzy Nim lay all over it, and ran all round it, and stopped to sharpen her claws on the elderberry, and hunch her back, and wash over her ear.

I, who may not do these things, looked around for something to dig, or pull up, or plant; something to knock to pieces, or nail together, but could find nothing. Something had to be done, and there was no wood to chop, so I collected all my boots and cleaned them. Next I started on the dark-room, and broke two dishes; overhauled the camera for leaks, and dusted the bottles and printing-frames. Just to see if this day was really as good as it looked, I put an old negative in the window to print, and in three-quarters of an hour there was quite a noticeable image on the paper.

These last three evenings we have spent over seed catalogues, saying one to another, "Wouldn't it be fine if they'd only come up like the pictures?"

Thinking it over, I seem to remember that most of these things happened last year. So I shall keep my thick overcoat hanging behind the door for a little while longer.

A Recipe for Youth

It would be interesting to know at what age one begins to grow old, where boyhood ceases. Certainly the opinion of the individual is of little account. He is always at the prime of life, just beginning his best work, and, honestly, he never felt better. Saying which, he smooths down his waistcoat as if he would flatten it a little, squares his shoulders, and maybe thumps you in the back to prove his light-heartedness. Maturity is no landmark; many men have not begun to learn to be boys until nearly thirty, and many never begin—poor fools.

I know a man who, when he married, hired a house overlooking a railway cutting, and spent his pleasantest hours, so he said, sitting on the garden wall, watching the trains and swinging his legs. He was a simple soul, and had he been certain of privacy I doubt not he would have waved a flag and blown a whistle. He knew the names of all the engines, and what time they were due at Grantham or Crewe. But for the fact that he was very careful, his friends might easily have put him in a lunatic asylum. Yet he made money by selling jute all day, and was a sound man on 'Change. He had simply forgotten to leave off being a boy; or did not recognise the time to do so when it came.

Games are no index either. We progress from cricket with piled coats for wicket to cricket with real stumps and pads; and when we grow too round to run or too bald to go hatless, we take up the more leisurely and philosophic golf. And in taking to golf do we not always do it by the doctor's orders? That is because, knowing we are fat and scant of breath, we are a little ashamed to be seen playing glorified marbles for no other purpose than mere pleasure. Golf is a sign of maturity; but it also shows that the boy in us is not dead, but very much alive and kicking against the bald head and growing waist measurement, kicking to be free again.

So long as there is a little bit of the human boy still with us we must play games, or collect stamps, or do something of which youth is supposed to have the monopoly. Thus do we try to persuade ourselves that we are not growing old.

If you possess a son or a nephew there is another method of testing your blood for traces of boyhood. Go to his box. It has rope handles, and its home is under his bed. His initials will be handsomely carved on the lid, the whole ornamented with brass-headed nails. You know what you will find in it; some fishing-hooks and lines, a float, a batting glove, "The Scalp Hunters," "Peter the Whaler," an air-pistol with bullets, "The Coral Island," "The Fifth Form at St. Dominic's," and a catapult. Now see what you can do with these.

The fishing lines, of course, are for all time; the air-pistol you can still use with satisfaction, and the catapult you think you could manage again with practice.

But the books! They are just the books you read at his age, lying on the hearthrug before the lamps were lit, in bed before the light was put out, and, if it were a very ripping yarn, in bed again before you were called to breakfast. You will remember your copy of "Coral Island," all dropping to pieces, with breadcrumbs in the binding, with tea-stains and butter-marks on its pages; your "Clipper of the Clouds," patched with stamp edging, and every page turned down. Have these that old power over you still? Can they keep you from the fleshpots? I have tried, alas! and found them tiresome; the lives of those old heroes are far too charmed, their escapes from death far too narrow. We bring a maturer judgment to bear on these things now, and are by no means so easily pleased. What once thrilled us as heroic we now find but empty bombast, what held us with the grip of the dramatic is to-day merely banal, what passed for humour just balderdash. This certainly looks as if our youth had slipped away from us, as if all the boy in us were dead. Our favourite hero no longer turns in his saddle to urge on his trusty followers with a wave of his scarlet sword, or leaps aboard the Frenchman before the gunwales have crunched together. Instead, he sits at a microscope and writes papers on heredity in house-flies, or

(Heaven help us!) squirms in a chair all bell-pushes, and controls empires and stock markets.

At forty it is hard to get an extra beat or two into the pulse, to quicken the dying boy; but it can be done. My elixir of life stands on the bottom shelf of my bookcase, eight fat volumes of the "B.O.P." I take the doses for preference on winter evenings; generous draughts, for every volume is a widow's cruse.

The very heroes who in book form made your gorge to rise just now, here where you first met them will surely colour your cheek again. You remember the weekly fight within yourself; should you buy the weekly parts with your weekly penny and put yourself out of your misery, or could you save the fourpence and buy the monthly part. If you decided on the latter and more heroic course, what a feast awaited you. What a reward for virtue! And thus only could you get the coveted coloured plate, British Moths, Flags of all Nations, the Death of Nelson, Uniforms of the British Army, Song Birds and their Eggs. Take up a volume now, you old men, and see whether the boy in you be dead and cold. Here are "My Friend Smith" and "The Adventures of a Three Guinea Watch." Dear old Talbot Baines Reed! You were thirty-five when you read of his death; but still you had to blow your nose until the tears welled into your eyes, as you told your boy of the draught you had been sitting in all day. Here, too, is that article on "How To Make and Work a Galanty Show." That kept you amused all one wet week, while the house was full of paper trimmings and the smell of glue. Or, may be, it is the wonderful first volume, with "From Powder Monkey to Admiral" in it. I am not old enough to have bought those numbers week by week, but later on uncle gave me the bound volume, after he had read it himself. How we hid in corners and shirked lessons that we might share the exploits of Will, Jack, and Oliver, break gaol with them, blow frigates out of the water with them, be marooned with them, and become admirals all with them.

Truly there is much good medicine in those back numbers. And in the present numbers, though I do not hope to convince you of that. Such institutions as the "B.O.P." are never anything like as good as they were in our day, are they? Of course not! The same thing applies to those good old-fashioned winters. Yet you must not forget your own weekly penny; you must see that your boy gets his much inferior "B.O.P." Then you can steal upstairs when he has gone to bed, and read in it yourself. Of course, you will pooh-pooh it, and snort at it, but you will love it in your heart, for it is just the same. If anything has altered it is yourself. You are now looking at life through the wrong end of the telescope. It must always be just the same, youth eternal, and health, and high spirits. The man whose chords do not vibrate in sympathy, whose blood has no surge left in it, who cannot even conjure a memory of his old self as he fingers the orange covers, that man is of no use. He is burnt out, and in a properly organised community he would be requested to step into a hot bath and open a vein.

Checklist of Issue Dates

The checklist below provides the original publication date in the *Morning Leader* for each of the sketches included in this collection.

"On Getting the Sack," October 28, 1905.

"On Looking for Work," November 2, 1905.

"On Going After a Place," November 8, 1905.

"The 'Last Workmen's'," January 8, 1906.

"The Staff Dinner," April 16, 1906.

"The Wandering Minstrels," August 7, 1906.

"A Night Out," February 28, 1907.

"A Winter Foreword," December 6, 1907.

"The Call of the Downs," April 10, 1908.

"A Night Awake," May 22, 1908.

"The River," June 12, 1908.

"Motley," August 25, 1908.

"The Pleasures of Hope," September 23, 1908.

"The Convalescent," November 19, 1908.

"The Art of Reading," December 18, 1908.

"Shop Windows," December 31, 1908.

" 'Mother Shippey's'," January 14, 1909.

"The Art of the Pipe," January 27, 1909.

"The Art of Dress," March 2, 1909.

"The Post," April 14, 1909.

"The Choice of a Profession," May 13, 1909.

"The South Country," June 3, 1909.

"On Being Barbered," June 24, 1909.

"The Luncheon Hour," July 20, 1909.

"Reading at Table," November 27, 1909.

"Of Uncles," March 12, 1910.

"Slippers," March 26, 1910.

"The Comforter," May 25, 1910.

"The Time Machine," July 29, 1910.

"Writing Home," September 2, 1910.

"Some Ancestors," March 20, 1911.

"Our Ship," October 19, 1911.

"The Awakening," March 5, 1912.

"A Recipe for Youth," April 10, 1912.

F. W. Thomas

An Appreciation

The first article by F. W. Thomas was published on October 28, 1905. "On Getting the Sack" was sold to the *Morning Leader*, a Liberal halfpenny daily founded in 1892 and published, along with the similarly radical *The Star*, from the newspaper's offices in Stonecutter Street, London, E.C.4. Other articles followed, and within a year Thomas had joined the editorial staff of the *Morning Leader*, working as a junior reporter under editor Ernest Parke, who was at the helm of both newspapers. In 1908 Thomas showed his editor a humorous sketch he had written, asking him what he thought of it. Although Parke deemed it unsuitable for publication, he recognised his gift for humour and encouraged him to keep at it. Notwithstanding this, Thomas' excellent sketches and articles continued to appear in the paper on a regular basis over the course of the next four years.

Thomas' fledgling journalistic career with the *Morning Leader* ended in 1912 when the title came under the ownership of the Cadbury family and was absorbed into the *Daily News* to form the new *Daily News and Leader*. The London evening newspaper *The Star*, the *Morning Leader*'s long-standing sister publication, was also purchased by the Cadbury family. In May of 1912 Thomas joined the staff of that paper in their new offices in Bouverie Street; his first article for *The Star* was printed on August 14 of the same year.

From the outset, Thomas was a frequent contributor to *The Star*, where he remained for over thirty years. During this time he wrote hundreds of humorous stories and sketches and a regular Monday column that was usually accompanied by the artwork of numerous *Star* illustrators.

Thomas' most famous collaboration in this vein was with the noted political cartoonist David Low. Their successful partnership resulted in the popular "Low and I" series which began in 1922 and lasted for five years. The many humorous articles they produced consisted of reports of their visits to a variety of locations in and around London. These included such places as the Monument, the Tower of London, Billingsgate Market, the Serpentine, London Zoo, Madame Tussauds and Sotheby's. The "Low and I" series spawned two books: *Low and I: A Cooked Tour in London* (1923) and *The Low and I Holiday Book* (1925).

It could be said that the success of the series rather obscured the fact that the two had a slightly uneasy relationship. On arriving at Fleet Street all the way from Australia (he was originally from New Zealand), Low had expected to be working on a national daily. Considering himself a genius, he was said to have been somewhat disappointed at his placement on a London evening newspaper. With Thomas nine years his senior and, as the native Londoner, very much taking the lead as regards their location-based assignments, a little of the tension due to their different backgrounds and personalities does come across in the "Low and I" sketches. But the marriage of their talents produced some fantastic work, and over the years they built up a genuine fondness for one another. When one was off sick or on holiday, the other would "hold the fort" by carrying on the feature alone until their return. Thomas himself had some artistic ability and would enjoy supplying his own quirky cartoons in Low's absence.

This highly successful series finally ended in 1927, when Low left to work on the *Evening Standard*. After Low's departure Thomas continued the feature for a few more years, teaming up with the *Star* artist who signed his work as "Gee."

Down the years, Thomas' work for *The Star* also included a varied selection of informal essays and feature articles. Among these latter were a memorable series of travelogues in which Thomas documented extended visits he made to Paris, New York, Chicago and South America. It was on the first leg of this last trip, the background to which I will discuss in more detail later on in this essay, that Thomas met Rudyard Kipling in January 1927.

By chance Kipling was sailing out of Southampton on the same ship as Thomas, the R.M.S.P. *Andes*, bound for Buenos Aires. The night before embarkation Thomas had got wind of the fact that Kipling would be on board, and wired his editor, as any good newspaperman would feel obliged to do. After they had set sail the next day, the purser informed Thomas that he had made a faux pas, in that Kipling preferred the public not to know when he was off on his travels. Thomas apologised to Kipling and, in so doing, broke the ice, with the latter assuring him that he need not worry (as he couldn't have known), and besides, in his profession he was meant to be on the lookout for anything considered newsworthy. The two went on to enjoy a number of conversations on their way across the Atlantic. Years later these discussions formed the subject of a memoir that Thomas published in *The Star* in 1936.

Having published the reports Thomas sent back about his South American trip in 1927, ten years later *The Star* commissioned him to write a series of travelogues about his visit to the U.S.A. in 1937. Thomas' candid observations on the cities of New York and Chicago were well received, and were followed up by a string of equally funny articles detailing his visit to Paris in August of the same year.

But despite the importance of his travel articles and collaborative work, the bulk of Thomas' output for *The Star* was in the form of humorous writings which, for the most part, appeared on a weekly basis. The F. W. Thomas "Saturday Short Story" was a staple of the paper for decades, prompting the author and journalist Gerald Gould to describe him as "the man who is Saturday"!

Thomas was a gifted writer, equipped with a vivid imagination, an ear for dialogue and an ability to view commonplace situations in a highly individual way. This last aspect was summed up perfectly by a critic writing in the *Saturday Review* in 1923: "The most ordinary incidents furnish him with occasions of tenderness and cheerfulness. Mr. Thomas is a friendly philosopher—he comforts."

His stories were indeed marked by their gentle wit, lightness of touch and incisive insights into what makes people tick. These qualities were apparent in the stories he wrote about everyday London life, whether they were meditations on people's habits when travelling on the Underground, tales of put-upon City office workers, or the series of comedies which featured his outrageous fictional creation "Pamela," a scatter-brained high society girl.

And then there were all those strange tales set in a faerie world of his own devising that for years proved popular with readers of *The Star*. Peopled with an endearing cast of elfin folk and magical beings, Thomas' delicate, whimsical tales of fantasy proved beyond doubt his incredible versatility as a writer.

Perhaps Thomas' most important work for *The Star* were his many rural sketches, which he used in part as a showcase for his obvious love of nature and deep affinity with the English countryside. Several of these tales featured recurring characters, verbose eccentrics such as Mr. Grindle the Cobbler, his fatuous neighbour Simpson, and a small army of innkeepers, hawkers, shopping ladies and railway porters. Through characters such as these, Thomas (who after all was a trained journalist) used his powers of observation to good effect, employing wry humour to comment on the habits and foibles of people in rustic settings. He would also utilise made-up place names in his stories; the localities described therein would therefore represent just about any part of the British countryside. This aspect helped to establish the universal appeal of his humour. It is these latter stories and sketches, in which Thomas, in his own quirky way, documents his many hikes across the rural landscape, be it Sussex, Devon, or elsewhere, that comprise the main body of his vast literary output.

His writings for *The Star* and *Daily News* in this vein were well represented in book collections of his work. Hundreds of Thomas' pieces for the newspapers were reprinted in various hardbound editions. These include the best-selling volumes *Extra Turns* (1917), which was reprinted several times, *Saturday Nights* (1923), *Cobbler's Wax* (1925) and *Windfalls* (1932). All of his books were well received, and met with widespread critical acclaim, as reviews in numerous periodicals at the time testify.

Perhaps the most high profile critique of one of his books was by J. B. Priestley, whose esteem for Thomas was evident in a favourable review he wrote about the collection *Week-Ends* (1925). An ardent admirer of Thomas, Priestley reflected on the appeal of his humorous sketches: "The tales and sketches are the thing. They all have good ideas, of the kind O. Henry would have made into short stories, and, what is more important, they have a personal humorous flavour, that drollery which is unanalysable like a flavour or a scent, on the telling. The phonetic spelling itself is a triumph of observation." Priestley also felt that Thomas should be taken seriously as a writer: "Writing of this kind needs something more than a comic fancy, it needs a man who keeps his eyes and ears open and has observation and memory at the service of his calling. It needs, in short, a serious writer. That, I think, is the secret of Mr. Thomas' success as a humorous journalist. He is seriously occupied with the business of writing. He gives his work, however light it may be, however extravagant, the flavour of literature. He is, like all successful humorists, a sober craftsman and a serious man."

These sentiments were in fact an echo of some of Thomas' own thoughts on his approach to writing. In a rare interview printed in 1924 in his local paper the *Chiswick Times*, Thomas offered the following insight: "Let me tell you, being humorous is anything but funny; it is one of the most serious things in life. Anyone can be serious because life itself is serious, and it is no use to sit down and be tragic because, again, all things in life are tragic, but being humorous is the most tragic thing of the lot. You have to swallow all your own beliefs and opinions about life in general and take up an entirely new personality. People come to the office to see me sometimes and are disappointed. I believe they have expected to see a man with a red nose and a humorous cast of countenance—a sort of cross between Harry Lauder and George Robey—and instead of that have found a serious-looking young gentleman. It takes quite a serious man to be a humorist. As proof of that we have Dan Leno, whose great ambition in life was to play Romeo, Charlie Chaplin desired to play Hamlet, and my great ambition is to write a really serious novel, to do some good in the world. But humour has become such an integral part of my life now that I doubt if I could do it."

Beyond the readership of the *Daily News* and *The Star*, some of his sketches and stories found an even wider audience when they appeared in magazines such as *Lilliput*, *Tit-Bits*, *John O'London's Weekly* and *The Passing Show*. Thomas also co-wrote a stage musical called "His Girl," which ran for two months at the Gaiety Theatre at Aldwych in 1922. This extra exposure went some way towards increasing his fame. And who knows if his popularity would have expanded even further had he accepted the offer of Lord Beaverbrook (owner of the *Daily Express* and *Evening Standard*) to switch allegiances and come work on one of his newspapers for a higher salary? It's interesting to note that his old colleague on *The Star* David Low did just that thing, whereas Thomas is said to have enjoyed turning Beaverbrook down!

Towards the end of his long career with *The Star*, Thomas increasingly focused his creative energies on writing poetry. Prior to this, many of his articles and sketches had contained a liberal sprinkling of playful songs and verses. But throughout the late 1920s and into the 1930s he contributed to the paper a quite impressive string of narrative, story-length ballads. Some of these humorous verses were later collected in the book *The Ballads of Barnacle Bill and Other Jingles* (1943).

In 1929 Thomas found a fresh forum for his delightfully lopsided view of the world when he began a new column in *The Star* called "News From Nowhere." Renamed "This Cock-Eyed World" (later "Cock-Eyed Corner") in 1937, this was a mixed bag of jokes, riddles, musings and overheard conversations. It appeared in *The Star* on a daily basis, and lasted into the early years of the Second World War, when the column, at least in part, took on a satirical tone. On a visit to Germany in August 1938, Thomas had seen with his own eyes the persecution of the Jewish population by Hitler's regime. In the early months of 1940, Thomas used the final entries in the "Cock-Eyed Corner" series to poke fun at the Nazi propaganda regime. He was particularly scathing of Goebbels and the lies perpetrated by German radio broadcasts.

The ridicule Thomas meted out in this column and other articles with *Star* caricaturist Fred Joss, taken together with his prominent position as a long-serving journalist on *The Star* and *Daily News* (two newspapers that for years had been critical of Hitler's rise to power and the whole Nazi ideology), led to Thomas being placed on the Nazi death list, in common with his former colleague, David Low.

"Cock-Eyed Corner" was gradually phased out in favour of other features. There were for instance the brilliant "At Home with the Militia" sketches he produced in partnership with *Star* artist Leslie Grimes in the days leading up to the outbreak of war. In each of these pieces Thomas and Grimes would "fall in" with the new recruits at a number of army bases and send back reports of military life that were both illuminating and funny at the same time.

Following on from this series, Grimes would continue to contribute his regular "All My Own Work" feature, which showcased his fine cartoons and artwork in *The Star* for many years. A First World War veteran who had served as an air pilot and infantryman, Grimes also achieved renown for being the only British newspaper artist to visit the Royal Air Force in France in the weeks prior to the Allied retreat at Dunkirk. His exclusive drawings for *The Star* were flown home courtesy of the R.A.F.!

Thomas' work with Grimes made way for what proved to be a longer lasting collaboration with the legendary Roy Ullyett, another outstanding *Star* artist famous for his work as a sports cartoonist. The dozens of inspired articles they produced together were conceived very much in the style of "Low and I" and entertained readers into the early years of the war. The series was cut short when Ullyett received his call-up papers, going on to serve in the R.A.F. before returning to newspaper work on being demobbed.

The first few months of the Second World War were a particularly prolific period for Thomas, even by his standards. Starting in November 1939 Thomas compered the "Stories of the Home Front" column. In this feature he invited readers to send in anecdotes relating to their experiences of home-made trenches, black-outs and air-raids.

This feature proved to be short-lived, however, and was ultimately superseded by a column that Thomas had much experience of writing. In addition to his prolific output for *The Star*, Thomas had conducted the long-running "Merry-Go-Round" column in the *Daily News* (renamed the *News Chronicle* in 1930) throughout the 1920s and 1930s. Not dissimilar to the "This Cock-Eyed World" column, this feature was supplanted to *The Star* during the Blitz of 1940. A fun-packed miscellany of jokes, trivia, puzzles and readers' letters,

"Merry-Go-Round" sadly fell victim to wartime restrictions on paper usage. As *The Star* itself shrank in page count, Thomas' column got smaller and smaller, until by the end of 1941 it had been phased out completely.

Among his very last contributions to *The Star* were the wartime sketches he wrote as part of the "From the Coastal Zone" series, which ran from 1941 to 1945. These humorous pieces told the story of everyday life in a small community on the Sussex Coast during the Second World War. The locale was obviously Thomas' hometown of Seaford in East Sussex, though for reasons of national security the exact location was not revealed at the time. This aspect would have come naturally to Thomas, as he had for years been apt to use made-up place names in most of his sketches and stories. The "From the Coastal Zone" series is of some historical interest today, detailing as it does the effect on a quiet seaside town of the sudden invasion of barracked troops, gun emplacements, barbed wire, food rationing and German air-raids. These unique and fascinating pieces remain highly readable today, over sixty years since they were originally published.

Thomas' final article for *The Star* appeared in November 1945. In "A Word to Mr. Wells" Thomas urged readers not to take all of H. G. Wells' predictions too seriously, arguing that while some had turned out to be accurate, others had not. Apparently the general mood of the nation at the time this article was written was one of gloom, and it's perhaps fitting that Thomas signed off from *The Star* by telling everybody to "cheer up"!

After his retirement from newspaper work, Thomas collaborated with *The Star* and *News Chronicle* illustrator James Francis Horrabin by contributing songs and verses for his "Japhet and Happy" cartoon annuals (he had previously written stories based on Horrabin's "Dot and Carrie" cartoon strip). From 1947 onwards Thomas worked as a book reviewer for the magazine *John O'London's Weekly*. His contributions to this periodical, which lasted until early 1953, also included several feature articles and the occasional humorous short story.

A very private man, throughout his long career as a Fleet Street newspaper journalist he was never given to talking much about himself. Hard biographical information about Thomas was rather thin on the ground, indeed virtually non-existent are far as his many readers at the time were concerned. Even at the height of his popularity, reviewers of his book collections would note that about the man himself, little was known to the public. One could glean certain odd snippets of information from his writings, and make educated guesses about just *who* F. W. Thomas the man was. Readers could infer his literary tastes (such as his fondness for Shakespeare and Keats), that he smoked a pipe, owned a dog, was a keen ornithologist, enjoyed long walks, country pubs, good conversation and was an eternally patient observer of people.

As for the biographical facts that we now know today, our knowledge of his early life is limited to scarce items of information. It is known that Frederick William Thomas was born in Hackney, London on January 14, 1882. His father was a merchant seaman who later worked as a fishmonger. His parents had several children, and although he grew up alongside his siblings in the family home in Hackney, both his maternal and paternal ancestral roots were centred in the Rye and Udimore districts of East Sussex.

Thomas attended a Board School in Hackney but left at the relatively early age of thirteen. An avid reader who was largely self-educated and had a good head for figures, as a young man he obtained work as an invoice clerk for a commercial concern in the City of London. Finding himself unemployed in 1905, he began submitting candid articles about his jobless plight to the *Morning Leader*. The editor did not hesitate to publish Thomas' wry and honestly written contributions, and within a year he had joined the paper as a clerk. Soon afterwards he secured a placement on the editorial staff of the *Morning Leader*. Interviewed in 1924, Thomas recalled the background to his joining the paper: "At that time I knew nothing about journalism, except that you must write on one side of the paper only and not split infinitives."

Around the time he joined *The Star* in 1912, Thomas got married and moved to Chiswick in West London. For 17 years Thomas commuted to the City from this suburb, where he lived with his wife

Louisa Augusta (nee Podbury) and their two children Margaret and Peter. Meanwhile, his writing career went from strength to strength.

The aforementioned trip that he made to South America, which resulted in several articles, had a background of personal tragedy. Thomas' son died in 1926 at the age of 11, and in January 1927, the proprietors of *The Star* and *Daily News* sent Thomas on sabbatical leave, while he came to terms with the loss of his beloved son. A news item in *The Star* was published on January 29, 1927, informing Thomas' many fans of his absence. The following extract reveals how important to the paper he was: "The fact is that F. W. Thomas has been getting a little bit under the weather, though you would never have suspected from his *Star* articles that he was what is commonly called 'run down.' Thomas will carry with him the good wishes not only of his colleagues, but of the many thousands of *Star* readers for his complete restoration to good health—and high spirits."

Ever the professional, Thomas had evidently been working through his grief, and one can surmise today that his fellow newspapermen on *The Star* and *Daily News* could see that both physically and mentally he was running himself into the ground.

On the orders of his editors, in late January 1927 Thomas boarded the R.M.S.P. *Andes*, setting off from Southampton on a sea voyage that would last several weeks and whose ultimate destination was Buenos Aires. It was on the trip across the English Channel to Cherbourg, during which Thomas had the previously discussed meeting with Rudyard Kipling, that he began to compose reports on his travel experiences, to be posted back to *The Star* at the next port of call. Continuing to write his letters home as the ship made its way across the Atlantic to Pernanbuco and then on to Rio de Janeiro and Montevideo, Thomas' entertaining missives began to appear in *The Star* in March of that year. Published while he was still away under the heading "Chasing the Sun," the articles he sent back described his long train journey across land from Buenos Aires to Valparaiso in Chile, and from there his second sea voyage aboard the R.M.S.P. *Oropesa*. Stopping off at various ports on the coast of Peru, this second vessel eventually brought Thomas through the Panama Canal and across the

Caribbean Sea via Jamaica, Havana, and finally Bermuda before re-crossing the Atlantic and arriving at Plymouth in early April.

His odyssey to South America having taken over two months, Thomas returned to the pages of both papers in April 1927. In somewhat sporadic fashion, David Low had continued the "Low and I" column in his absence. Thomas wasted little time in teaming up again with his long-term colleague, while over at the *Daily News*, he resumed his weekly "Merry-Go-Round" feature, which Ashley Sterne had ably conducted while he was away. With his customary "Saturday Short Story" appearing every week, a revitalised Thomas was back on form in no time.

Two years later the pull of his family heritage proved too strong to resist, and in 1929 he and his wife relocated to East Sussex; a region where he spent the remainder of his days. Writing from his home on the South Downs, he regularly sent in his copy to the London offices of *The Star* and *Daily News*, occasionally dropping in to the Bouverie Street headquarters on visits to London.

Facts such as these, however, would not have been revealed to his readers at the time. What was known of Thomas as a journalist and humorist far outweighed the knowledge they would have had of his personal life, particularly in the final years of his career with *The Star*. To such an extent, in fact, that after his last piece appeared in a November 1945 issue of the paper, to the public at large, no more was heard of Thomas. True, if one happened to read *John O'London's Weekly*, or see his name on Horrabin's "Japhet and Happy" annuals, one would have been aware of his post-war output. But neither *The Star* nor the *News Chronicle* carried any announcements of his retirement and certainly no acknowledgement whatsoever that his long newspaper career had come to an end. Back then, his faithful readership on the paper would have been left wondering what had happened to him. It should be noted, though, that all this mystery was admittedly in keeping with the author's long-standing and carefully maintained privacy.

From my own point of view, having discovered his work so many years after he was famous, for a long time I pondered on the mystery of what had become of Thomas after 1945. This enigma lasted until very recently, when a genealogical researcher friend of mine managed to uncover various items of vital biographical information, such as his date of birth. And then, by coincidence, shortly after this I was contacted by Thomas' grandchildren, who acknowledged certain facts already guessed at and revealed much more relating to his life after 1945.

Thomas lived out much of his retirement at his home in the East Sussex seaside town of Seaford, where he had lived since 1929. After his wife died in 1961, he finally settled with his daughter's family in the village of Old Heathfield. During the remaining years of his life Thomas served as honorary treasurer of the Searchlight Cripples' Workshops in Newhaven, an organisation partly aimed at helping disabled war veterans. He remained an avid reader and enjoyed gardening, archaeology, wildlife and sitting in his greenhouse, thinking and dreaming away the hours. Thomas was immensely fond of his three grandchildren and was apt to entertain them with his poems, cartoons, and beautifully constructed models of villages, complete with ponds, churches, and hedges, etc.

Much loved by all of his family, he passed away at his home aged 84 on October 3, 1966. Among those who attended his funeral was Arthur Webb, an old colleague from *The Star*. Obituaries for Thomas were printed in *The Times* and his local paper the *Sussex Express*.

And so the biographical information and insights kindly supplied by Thomas' grandchildren now help to shape our understanding of his autumn years. With this newly acquired knowledge, one can only hope against hope that the day will come when more readers will discover the brilliant works of this talented writer. His legacy of varied writings is surely long overdue for a revival.

For now, I offer to the modern reader these new collections of his work, bringing F. W. Thomas' unique brand of humour and observational talents into the light once again.

Richard Simms
Surrey, England
February, 2010

Further Reading

The long career F. W. Thomas had with *The Star* is discussed in more depth in the essay "F. W. Thomas: Star Man," published on the internet at the following web address:

http://thestarfictionindex.atwebpages.com/f_w.htm

The same website also contains a comprehensive checklist of the short stories and fictional sketches Thomas contributed to *The Star* from 1912 through 1945.

www.ingramcontent.com/pod-product-compliance
Lightning Source LLC
Chambersburg PA
CBHW020141180626
46810CB00004B/1672